Ring
Of
Gyges

Written and Illustrated

by

A. Wales

𝔄𝔚some 𝔅ooks

First published in Great Britain in 2001 by
AWsome Books, 1 Wide Lane Close, Brockenhurst SO42 7TU

Copyright © 2001 A. Wales

ISBN 0 9539904 1 9

Printed in Great Britain by El Alamein Press Ltd, Salisbury

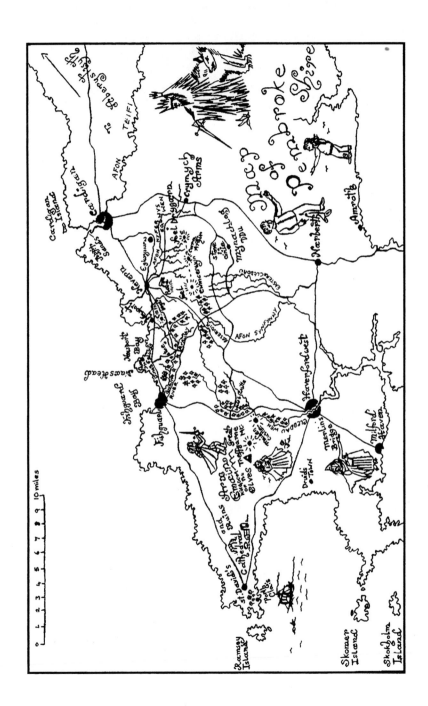

MAP of PEMBROKE Shire

0 1 2 3 4 5 6 7 8 9 10 miles

THE TRILOGY

The Stone, The Ring and The Shield

PART I
The Stone of Gardar

PART II
The Ring of Gyges

PART III
The Shield of Agamemnon

PART II

The Ring of Gyges

With Best Wishes
from

Ann Wales.

Happy Reading
2003!

PREFACE

The Stone, The Ring and The Shield

It all began with a stone from St. David's, a large volume in Ancient Welsh from Aberystwyth University, and Peter and Sarah, who have been wanting me to tell their story for at least the last thirty years. My two shadow children had been with me ever since I began writing stories at school. They came into being properly during the family holidays in Wales.

Pembrokeshire, the Prescelly Mountains in particular, is a very strange place, with ancient monuments strewn around every few yards. One can well imagine that Elves or, in Welsh, *Ellyllon*, the Family of Beauty, are never far away. I always wanted to meet them and Peter and Sarah, through the power of the miraculous stone are able to do so.

The stories are rooted in a strong family background. We first meet the children with their Aunt Myfanwy (Aunt Myf) who usually has them for the summer holidays, while the children's archaeologist parents teach at University summer schools. Peter and Sarah are taken to visit St. David's and it is there that Peter discovers a strange looking stone, it is the *Stone of Gardar*. Little does he realise that it is a long lost treasure of the Elves of Arx Emain, a stone of great power and a portal to other dimensions. It is then that the adventures really begin!

The first book of this trilogy concerns the continuing battle for Power between Gwyn-ap-Nudd, King of Arx Emain and Lord of the Elves, and Arddu, the Dark One. The ancient Stone of Gardar could be an aid to either side. Its discovery by Peter is a vital element of the struggle.

When the war between the Elves and their adversaries is over, Peter and Sarah's Mother and Father, Dr. and Mrs. Jones, are brought to Wales. They meet Anir who is a long lost relation of Peter and Sarah's Mother and their Aunt Myf. He is the Guardian of the lands around Arx Emain (the magical realm of Gwyn-ap-Nudd). He accompanies Peter and Sarah on many of their adventures in his capacity as envoy between humankind and the world of magic.

During the course of the trilogy, the whole Jones family enlarges and evolves and strengthens its bonds. As archaeologists, Mother and Father Jones are frequently busy on 'digs' around the world, often in Classical Lands. Peter and Sarah often travel with them, enabling them to discover the ties between history, magic and mythology. Whenever ancient monsters are disturbed, they know they can rely on the Elves and their friends to help them out. As the miraculous Stone of Gardar makes time travel possible, the children meet many heroes from ancient times.

In book two, we are introduced to Merlin and King Arthur, inhabitants of Roman Britain! Peter and Sarah are called out of their own time to try and help King Arthur win a war against the Western Roman Empire, aided by the ring of concealment, *The Ring of Gyges*.

Book three opens as Sarah and Peter travel to Greece with mother and father. Dr. Jones is working on a 'dig' at Mycene. Peter and Sarah have fun at a beach resort with their cousins Emma and Amy.

Father Jones discovers the tomb of a warrior and much treasure including *The Shield of Agamemnon*. However, the 'dig' awakens Agamemnon, Cassandra and Demeter. Disastrously, Demeter follows the treasure back to Wales when the family returns home. It takes all the wit and power of Merlin, the Elves and their miraculous stone to defeat her.

I am afraid Merlin had to make a return appearance because Peter and Sarah think he is so nice and they have got to like him! He also insists on re-appearing in some of the other stories.

Whatever does happen in the following books, the Jones family will find it interesting, exciting and exhilarating, and I am sure that my young readers will again find it gripping, entertaining and enjoyable!

CHAPTER ONE

A Surprise Meeting

It was Sarah's birthday. Sarah had looked forward to her
special day for weeks. She had hinted at the presents that would
please her most and nods and winks from Mother, Father and
Peter her brother gave her confidence that all her dearest dreams
would be fulfilled. As her birthday fell this particular year upon a
school day, a treat had been mooted for her return home. Father
had said the magic words *Burger Restaurant*. Yes, for the last

several days excitement had risen to fever pitch, only to be rewarded with the present, huge disappointment.

"Of all the mean tricks for fate to play!" thought Sarah, as she blew her nose loudly, coughed and wriggled further down in her bed.

In the next room she heard Peter give an answering cough and an absolutely humungous sneeze. Two days ago they had both felt fine and then, overnight, the local 'flu bug had laid them low. Sarah shut her eyes. She had a headache and a sore throat and Peter was no better off. From her nest under the duvet Sarah peeked at her presents and cards which presently adorned her desk. Mother and Father had given her a necklace of silver with turquoise beads and a blue velvet jewel case to keep it in.

Grandmother, who lived in London, had sent her a Murder Mystery board game and although she was too tired to even think about playing it, she very much looked forward to sharing it with Peter. Peter had given her a beanie toy. It was a cuddly dog that she had secretly admired in the local shop for weeks. Aunt Myf and Uncle Tomos had not been round as yet. While Sarah pondered on this, as if on cue, the front door bell rang and she heard voices in the hall.

"Yes, yes," she heard Mother say, "yes, they are still both poorly in bed."

"Well, I won't come in," Sarah heard Aunt Myf's voice float up the stairs, "but just give this to Sarah from all of us. Wish her *many happies*, give her a big kiss and say I'm sorry she's ill. I do hope all of you are better soon."

In the distance a baby began to wail.

"Look, that's Catrin yelling again," said Aunt Myf, "I must go. It's nearly her lunch time and I mustn't stay too long in case I catch your bugs and give them to baby."

Sarah heard footsteps leaving the house and the sound of a car going up the drive.

"I wonder what she has brought me?" thought Sarah.

The front door slammed and footsteps soon came slapping up the stairs. Mother put her head round the door and then came in, bearing a very large box.

"This is a very happy birthday from your Aunty Myfanwy," Mother said, placing the present on the bed in front of Sarah.

It looked most 'ticing! The box was wrapped in iridescent, holographic silver paper, with silver, white and pale blue ribbons tied round it. A large card lay on the top. Sarah ripped open the card and placed the beautiful picture of a white horse to one side. Then she soon had the box out of its coverings and open to reveal:

"A fleece! Wow! Ooooh Great! Just what I really wanted," Sarah hugged the garment to her.

"You'll look like a sheep in it," remarked Mother, as she removed the box and paper.

"No I shan't," said Sarah, "it's really *cool* and as it's white, it will go with *all* my clothes."

Sarah spread the fleece over the bed as an extra cover. Peter crawled out of bed and came to see what the commotion was all about

"Hi Sis," he whispered, "great fleece, really *cool*."

Then he retired back to his bed while Sarah made herself comfortable under her new fashion statement. Mother smiled a knowing smile as she went downstairs to prepare the birthday lunch for invalids.

The rest of Sarah's special day was a pleasant, if rather quiet one. Father came home early from the University for the ceremony of the birthday tea, but nothing else extraordinary or exciting happened. It had to be admitted, the fleece from Aunt Myf had been the high point of the day.

"I'll phone her of course, tomorrow when I'm feeling better," Sarah said to Mother when she came up to say Good night!

As she listened to Mother's good night visit to Peter and her return to Father and the grown-up world downstairs, Sarah mused to herself:

"I suppose nothing exciting will happen now for ages and ages; not until Christmas anyway."

She prepared for sleep, but as she did so, thought over the year that was past. It had been a lucky year for the Jones family.

"Ever since we met the Elves," she whispered, "I wonder what they are doing now? I'd love to find out what has happened at Arx Emain and how Anir and Aneryn are these days. I suppose they must get quite bored with no evil monsters to fight, now that Arddu is defeated... and the Lord Gwynn-ap-Nudd; does he just sit there in those Halls of Stone, watching the Stone of Gardar?"

Sarah began to cast her mind back to last year, when she and Peter had taken part in Elvish business of the most magical, mysterious and often quite frightening kind. Unfortunately her train of thought did not proceed much further as she fell directly off to sleep.

Next morning Sarah was beginning to feel just a little better, but Peter was worse.

"Perhaps it's 'flu AND pneumonia," Sarah said rather unhelpfully .

The Doctor was summoned, tablets were prescribed, and Mother fussed round Peter for the rest of that day and most of the following night. Sarah felt left out. During the afternoon she got out of bed for a while and aimlessly tidied her room. It was then that she once again put her hand on the ring that Anir had given her; the Ring of Concealment.

Since their adventure last summer, she had kept the ring in her jewel box. It lay forgotten at the bottom of the ring tray. As she moved her necklaces and bracelets, Sarah saw it glinting gold and pulled it out. During the great battle with Arddu it had kept her invisible and safe.

"I wonder," Sarah thought to herself, "I wonder if it still works?"

She took the ring from the tray and slipped it on her finger. Then she turned the great jewel into the palm of her hand.

"Am I invisible?" she shot a glance into her mirror.

No, there was no reflection! It was very weird and most disturbing. Sarah did not like it, so she tried something else. She tiptoed into Peter's room. No reflection there either.

"I *must* be invisible," Sarah thought.

Unfortunately Peter was asleep so there was no asking him.

"He does look ill though, poor thing," she thought, as he lay there looking extremely pale.

Beads of sweat glistened on his forehead.

"Poor Peter," Sarah patted his hand and he stirred a little. Again, footsteps could be heard on the stairs.

"It's Mum, bother!"

Sarah darted back into her room and put the ring back in its place. Strangely enough, she had never thought to put it on at home before today. Her reflection showed itself again comfortingly, back in its usual form.

"Hello face, nice to see you again," Sarah whispered, and got back into bed.

"Are you all right?" said Mother, poking her head round the door.

"Fine thanks," Sarah replied, and Mother went into Peter's room.

Sarah's brain by this time was seething with all sorts of extraordinary thoughts and plans. The Elves forming the greater part of them. When she fell asleep that night, she did so wondering if tomorrow Peter might be well enough to share the thoughts that were growing stronger and stronger within her brain, almost *unasked*... She wondered if he too wished that the Elves might contact them again... and also why on earth she did so herself!

"Anyway, at least he might tell me if the ring really works," she whispered, and passed into dreams of Arx Emain and the Elves within it.

Next morning Sarah woke with a start, as if someone called her name. She sat up in bed and rubbed her eyes awake. No, she was not dreaming. Someone was calling her name and that someone must be calling from outside and not inside the cottage. The pale glimmer of dawn showed through the gap in the curtains. No-one else seemed to be awake. Sarah sprang to the window. Two very small pebbles rattled briefly on her window pane. Sarah heard the voice call again,

"Sarah, Sarah!"

Quickly she fumbled with the catch and threw open the window. Leaning out she caught sight of a grey figure by the hedge.

"Sarah!" the figure said in a loud whisper, "we have been calling you these many days. We *must* meet. I shall wait for you and Peter by the Stones."

Then the shadowy figure disappeared into the bushes without giving Sarah any time to reply. A thrill went up and down her spine.

"Ederyn," she said, "I'm sure it was Ederyn!" then, "bother!" she said, "he's gone and I don't know what he meant. What stones?"

This was not an unreasonable query, for Wales is full of stones: mountains, rocks, cairns and standing stones at every turn.

Mother and Father began to get up and Peter was stirring. Sarah went to see how he was.

"Hello, how do you feel?" she asked.

16

"OK, I guess," her brother replied in a husky voice.

He did look a little better it was true.

"How are you, Sis?"

"Oh me, I'm fine," smiled Sarah, "I'm a bit wobbly in the legs but I think I'm on the mend."

"I think I'm over the hump of it too," said Peter, "But look here; I'm sure I heard you talking to someone earlier. Mum and Dad are only just awake, so unless you have the first sign of madness..."

"You mean talking to myself? No, I wasn't doing that."

Peter's eyes sparkled with intense curiosity and he half sat up; excitement lending him strength.

"Then you were talking to person or persons unknown. I knew it! I heard you open the window too. Who was it?"

"I think," said Sarah thoughtfully, "I think it was Ederyn."

"Ederyn!" said Peter, falling back on the pillows; his face flushed with pleasure, temperature, or both. "What on earth, or under it, did he want?"

"He wants to see us. He said that he had been calling us. Then he said:

"We must meet... I shall wait for you and Peter by the Stones."

"Hmmm," said Peter, puzzled, "what did he mean by *the stones* ?"

"Exactly," replied Sarah, "at the moment I can't imagine. It needs thinking about, but not now, here's Mum."

Sarah sat down on Peter's bed just as Mother appeared with Peter's breakfast tray and a thermometer. After she had satisfied herself that Peter's temperature was definitely on it's way down, she shooed Sarah away into her own room and took her temperature too.

"Cold, quite cold," said Mother, "thank goodness at least one of you is nearly back to normal."

She whisked herself downstairs and returned with Sarah's breakfast.

"Enjoy darling, I'll be back shortly," and she left to clear up downstairs.

All through breakfast Peter and Sarah silently pondered the message from the Elf Lord. What and where were the stones that he had mentioned? It was all very curious. Then Peter had another thought. When were they to meet Ederyn and worse still, how? Since their wild adventure with the Elves last year, Mother and Father were disinclined to let them out of their sight for more than two minutes.

"We'll never get away," he thought dismally, "even if we do find out where and what the Stones are."

He suddenly felt that he must get to see the Elves, whatever it might take to achieve this. Then he brightened suddenly with a new thought:

"Ah, isn't there a standing stone at Dinas?" he said to himself, and smiled.

Mother came to fetch the breakfast trays.

"Now then," she said to each of them, "be good this morning and if, I say IF you feel well enough, you might get to watch some television this afternoon. I'm going to be in the office typing some work up for your Father. He'll be away at the University until late; today and tomorrow. Something to do with his PhD Students he said. So *please* be good boys and girls, and Sarah, do telephone to thank Aunt Myf."

"We'll be very, very good," they said and Mother returned downstairs to wash up breakfast things and begin typing up a lecture on Ancient Celtic Lifestyles of the Iron Age.

She found the work very interesting and was so happy to be typing things about such fascinating people, she was soon lost to the world and back in prehistoric Britain.

As soon as Sarah thought that Mother was safely settled at the computer keyboard, she got up and tiptoed into Peter's room.

"All OK ?" she asked.

"Not too bad," said her brother, "but I've still got a bit of a headache with this temperature, so I can't guarantee that I'll come up with any genius solution this morning."

"Never mind," Sarah said, sitting down on the end of his bed. "Any thoughts so far?"

"Well," Peter began, "there's the standing stone at Dinas."

"But there are standing stones absolutely everywhere round here," Sarah protested. "No, I don't think it's that. Anyway, Ederyn said *stones* not stone. I wondered if he meant Pentre Ifan."

Peter tried to think. He shut his eyes and was so quiet for several minutes that Sarah began to wonder if he had gone to sleep. In the distant study they could hear Mother tap, tap, tapping on the computer keys. At last Peter sighed and said:

"I don't think it's Pentre Ifan either. Pentre Ifan is the remains of a burial chamber and comprises some very large stones, but I just don't think it's there Ederyn wants us to go."

"Then where does he mean?" Sarah looked completely mystified.

"You're quite sure that it was Ederyn?" Peter said suddenly.

"Of course I am sure. I'd recognise that voice anywhere."

"Well, in that case, I'll hazard a guess that he means Carn Ingli."

"Of course !" Sarah cried, clapping her hands together, but not too loudly that Mother might hear from downstairs, "that's it!"

"I've been thinking," said Peter, "you know, when we saw him for the first time it was not on the beach. THAT was the second time that we saw him. The first time we ever saw Ederyn was up at Carn Ingli, when we chased him and he just disappeared among the stones."

"Yes," agreed Sarah eagerly, "and he told us later that he was sent there as a lookout. Perhaps he goes there often."

"Quite! And so that is why I think that Carn Ingli has the stones we need to look for."

"But when shall we meet him and how can we get away?"

"Indeed, that's just what I have been thinking. But now I feel tired again. I think, Sarah dear, that I need to be asleep."

Peter shut his eyes again, then opened them again wide. "Before you go, Sis, do pour me some lemon barley water please." Sarah did so and gave him the glass. Peter drank it down, turned over in bed and slept again. Sarah tiptoed back to her room. Even if Carn Ingli was the right meeting place, the when and how of it escaped her entirely, so she gave it up. She snatched a book from the shelf by her door and read furiously until lunchtime.

After luncheon, Sarah telephoned to Aunt Myf to thank her for the fleece. She was treated to a long conversation, largely to do with babies, gardening and clothes, but not necessarily in that order! After that the day passed quietly, the following day too and several days more. Peter eventually lost the temperature and was allowed to join Sarah and inhabit the sitting room where they could watch television. Mother made them comfy on the settees and chairs and they were quite content to hibernate there for the following week. Then, on Friday afternoon, the Doctor made his last visit.

"Fit as two fleas!" he commented as he went out of the front door, "send 'em both back to school."

Sarah and Peter were listening upstairs and groaned at the thought.

"But there's only another week before we're off on Christmas holidays," complained Sarah.

"I think I feel a relapse coming on," said Peter.

Mother laughed.

"I thought that the last week of term before Christmas was always the best. Anyway, I have so much to catch up with, that I don't know where to start. I must do some Christmas shopping. I have been the Slave of the Bedroom Tray for too long. Make your minds up dears, it's school on Monday."

The weekend positively flew. Monday arrived and Father dropped them off at school in the car instead of walking.

"Can't have you ill again," he smiled.

They waved him goodbye as he sped off to work. In a way it was good to be back and they found the week at school was going to be fun. On Tuesday, there was a specially cooked Christmas Dinner, then on Wednesday, a visit to a local pantomime: Puss in Boots, then finally on Friday afternoon, there was the school carol concert. All pupils were obliged to participate in this and most parents were supposed to attend. This particular year it had been decided that the whole school was to perform at St. David's Cathedral.

"A very great honour for the school," their teachers kept telling them.

Peter and Sarah began to be rather pleased that they had not missed this event. Mother and Father would come of course. Father had already broken up from the University on the Wednesday afternoon and said that he was looking forward to hearing them sing. Mother always enjoyed things like carol concerts and this time she had asked Aunt Myf and Uncle Tomos and Catrin to come along too. However, it was just possible that Catrin might go to stay with Aunt Myf's neighbour for the occasion.

Friday afternoon arrived. After school dinners, all the children were put on to coaches and driven away to St. David's. All the parents were to arrive at the cathedral by two o'clock. Peter and Sarah's coach was the first to arrive at the Cathedral. All the children were marshalled out of the coach and into the beautiful church. As Sarah walked towards the front door, she thought she saw someone moving over by the ruins. No, it could not be, or could it? There was no time for a better look as her teacher ushered them to their seats at the front of the cathedral.

The pews filled quickly. Luckily, Peter was sitting next to Sarah. She whispered to him out of the side of her mouth:

"I think I just saw Ederyn."

"What!?"

"I think I just saw Ederyn. Don't you see, we've found *The Stones*! He was talking about the ruins of the Bishop's Palace."

Sarah had to break off, as one of the teachers had noticed her whispers, glared and said:

"No talking children, please!"

The parents arrived. By twisting slightly sideways, Peter could just see Mother, Father, Uncle Tomos and Aunt Myf. They had left Catrin behind. His mind returned to the problem of how to snatch a moment to talk with Ederyn. The first carol began. One of the older boys started them off in: Once in Royal David's City and managed the first verse quite well. The service was under way. Peter and Sarah's class sang the third carol: Silent Night, Holy Night.

"Very nice too," smiled Mother, as she made herself more comfortable in the pew.

She closed her eyes and let the music, children's voices and thoughts of Christmas wash over her.

At the end of the service the Head Teacher gave an address, before prayers led by the Bishop. During the address, Peter gave Sarah a dig in the ribs. She jumped in surprise, and stared at him crossly. Peter gave her a large wink of the eye to let her know that a plan was forming in his head.

The carol service ended and parents and children filed out of the Cathedral to shake the Bishop and Head Teacher by the hand. Then filled with all the hope and excitement that comes with the week before Christmas, the congregation prepared to go home for the holidays. Most of the children were going home with their parents. Only one of the coaches was going back to school with teachers and those whose parents had been unable to come. Fortunately there were very few of these.

As Peter and Sarah passed the massive Christmas Tree just inside the Cathedral doors, Peter grabbed Sarah's arm.

"Look, you or I have got to talk to Ederyn, or whoever it is."

"You do it Peter, you'll know what to say better than I will."

"Well then, you make some kind of distraction to give me enough time to see what's what, OK? Can you think of something?"

"Yes, I suppose so."

"Good girl! Give me at least ten minutes. Synchronise watches: it is now three ten and thirty seconds."

Peter and Sarah always enjoyed being scientifically precise on these occasions.

"OK Peter, I've got the time."

"Then off I go."

"Good luck!"

Sarah watched as Peter slunk into the shadows outside. Her mind was a whirl of ideas.

"I know, I'll ask them all to come and look at the tree, and I think I saw a very nice crib at the front of the Lady Chapel. I'll say that I simply must have a closer look."

With this in mind, Sarah went to shake hands with the Bishop.

It was about five minutes into *secret meeting time*, that Sarah actually found the rest of the family. Being congratulated on the performance of the carols by herself and Peter, even though it had been minimal, took at least another five minutes. Then, before anyone could ask where Peter was, Sarah had dragged them all down to the front of the Cathedral to view the crib, which was VERY nice indeed. Then it was off to the Tree, which they all proclaimed to be most beautiful. All this took nearly another ten minutes and before Mother could say:

"Where's your brother?"

Peter appeared before them from behind a pillar and the congratulations began again, until Aunt Myf kissed them both and said she simply must get back to collect Catrin. Uncle Tomos agreed and they departed, smiling and beaming.

"Now then," said Father, "let's find the car and it's home for the holidays. Although I don't think you two deserve any. You have had enough holiday already."

"Oh Daddy!" cried Peter and Sarah, "you are such a tease!"

"And it was 'flu not a holiday," Sarah told him, returning the tease. "We just opened the door and in-flu-enza !"

"No kidding!" said Peter, and after that there were more jokes and much laughter all the way home.

In the car, Sarah tried to ask Peter what had happened at St. David's. Had he seen Ederyn? If so, what had passed between them? She was dying to find out, but only received a wink and a grin with:

"I'll tell you later," from her annoying brother.

A celebratory supper was enjoyed by them all. Mother pulled out all the stops and gave the family Welsh lamb casserole, followed by pancakes and syrup. They all watched some television until Father called *time,* and then it was upstairs for bath and bed. Peter and Sarah bathed, cleaned teeth and were bade goodnight. The lights were turned off and Mother and Father went downstairs again to the television to relax with a detective thriller.

"Now for a chat with Peter," thought Sarah, "finally and at last! I'm just bursting to know what happened!"

Her own lust for adventure began to raise its ugly head just a tiny, little bit and *just in case...* she reached into her jewellery box and took with her the Ring of Concealment.

24

Then, as quietly as anybody could, Sarah tiptoed across the landing and into Peter's room.

"Hi there Sis!" said Peter, "are you ready?"

"I jolly well am, brother mine, so tell!"

"OK then; it was Ederyn!"

"I knew it."

"He was hiding just behind the Cathedral. I ran as fast as I could and we went over to the Bishop's Palace ruins to talk.

"Gwynn-ap-Nudd needs your help," he said.

"Our help?" I said.

"Yes, he requires the Ring that Anir gave your sister, the one that kept her safe during our last battle. Someone, perhaps **you** Peter, or both of you if Sarah likes, may be required to go with it, depending..."

"Depending on what?" I said, "and when shall we come, and how?"

"You will see. All shall be explained when you make your visit. You do not need to come immediately, for we want you to think seriously about this, but it must be before spring becomes summer. Enjoy the sacred time that lies before you in this present year and we shall hope to see you in the next."

"Oh, in the new year?" I said.

"Indeed, and as to how you come to us, well, we can find a way to do that I am sure. I think, Peter, that *you especially* may like the idea of the adventure that is planned. Now go... return to your celebrations. Give our greeting to your sister and tell her that we look forward to seeing you both in Arx Emain. Farewell!"

Then as soon as he had said that, he disappeared into the shadow of the ruins. I ran back to the Cathedral and you and the others were just coming down the nave."

Sarah squeezed her hands together with excitement.

"Another adventure! Oh goodeeee!"

"I thought you didn't like them."

"Well, I can change my mind if I like, can't I ?"

"Oh yes, certainly you can, on account of you're a girl!" Peter said scornfully.

"But I'm very curious to know what it is all about now. And anyway, I shan't mind going if it's a nice, little adventure," his sister told him, "just as long as there aren't any battles."

Peter was thinking of Sarah's many complaints during their last time with the Elves. She had often had to be extremely brave. She had also demonstrated an astonishing ingenuity and inventiveness under difficult circumstances, but then there was also her absolute terror during the battle between the Elves and Arddu.

Rightly so, now he came to think of it, for he had been totally terrified too. Even though wielding the Gardar Stone had given him something to occupy his mind, it had all been quite an ordeal. Indeed, he had been standing right by Anir when *The Guardian* had made the fatal thrust with his two handed sword, right into the chest of Arddu. However, that was all in the past now. Gwynn-ap-Nudd could not possibly have anything like that in mind again... could he?

"You'd better go back to bed, little sister."

"I will, but will you stop calling me 'little sister', I might be your sister, but I'm not LITTLE!" Sarah scowled.

"OK, OK, keep your hair on! We'll talk about this another time. No hurry, Ederyn obviously doesn't expect anything to happen until after Christmas."

"Good! I can go on making my shopping list then. Sleep well Peter."

"Goodnight Sarah," Peter yawned.

Sarah returned to her room and put the ring away in its place. "I wonder why they want it back now?" she said softly to herself.

She was certainly most curious by now, but after thinking for a moment she said to herself, very firmly and positively:

26

"Well, I just hope that it is Peter they want to wear the ring on their beastly adventure and not me. I'm not sure that I like being invisible anyway."

Then she got into bed and fell asleep.

CHAPTER TWO

To Arx Emain Again

"That was the best Christmas ever!" sighed Peter, as he pushed a very empty plate away.

They had just finished dinner on Boxing Day.

"Not forgetting last year!" interrupted Mother.

"Or next year!" said Father.

"Well, it's been very, very good," Peter said again.

"Brill!" agreed Sarah.

For so it had been. Pre-Christmas they had all gone up to the University one evening for drinks and nibbles, as Sarah put it.

"Canapés," Mother had corrected her, "small eats or nibbles are called *Canapés*, French, you know!"

The Master always gave a party for everyone on the staff and their families just before Christmas. Peter and Sarah adored it. They were all welcomed into a large room with many armchairs, sofas and tables in it. A huge fire roared in an ancient grate and in one corner stood the most magnificent Christmas tree that they had ever seen. Not only was the tree extremely well adorned, but it had *real* candles instead of the usual electric lights.

"How on earth it does not catch fire, I shall never know," said Mother.

"The Master has had a tree like this every year since he came to the University, so I am told," Father informed her.

"You had better keep well clear of the tree to be safe," he warned Peter and Sarah, "we don't want the fire brigade called out tonight, do we!"

But Peter and Sarah were quite happy to eat the eats and drink cola and lemonade, while admiring the flickering candle light and ignoring all the Grown-ups present. However, Peter did notice the presence of a fire extinguisher in the corner opposite the tree.

Christmas Eve arrived and after all the usual preparations were done, they all went to the Midnight service as usual. All sang the old favourite carols in full voice and returned home tired but joyful!

Christmas Day luncheon was provided by Aunt Myf, after the morning's feast of stockings and family presents. She felt that she and her sister should take turns at doing the cooking, now that they both had families. Then the Pantomime had enlivened Boxing Day afternoon and another huge meal had made the day complete. All the family felt as content as anyone can possibly be.

The following week provided the children with snow to play in. Whatever could be better than that! It was deeply satisfying to be able to ambush school friends in the village with unsuspected, well aimed snow balls. It was also wonderful to go tobogganing on Mother's best tea tray.

"It was the best at sledging and the biggest tray!" said Peter when Mother found out.

The snow was quite thick enough, also, to make a decent sized snowman. When they came indoors they hibernated over the television. Then, at the end of the holiday Father took them to see: *Inspector Inventor,* which was one of the films playing at the local cinema over Christmas.

All too soon the holidays were over and school began again. Father returned to the writing of lectures and the plan for a projected *dig* for the summer. Whenever Peter and Sarah's father, Dr. Jones, went on a dig, there always had to be a plan, forms to fill in and mountains more paperwork to do with it.

"Where is that?" asked Peter, when he saw the drawings and diagrams.

"Rome!" said Father grandly.

"Rome? Really and truly?"

"Yes, some people are going to dig up the floor in one of the very old churches to see what lies under it. Some of the local archaeologists think there may be an even earlier building underneath. A temple or villa perhaps. The Romans were always building new buildings on top of the old ones. A few of my final year students are helping to make up the team."

"Are you going as well?"

"Of course, and so are you."

"Wow!" exclaimed Peter.

"Yes, we are all going. It will be a nice summer holiday for you and very interesting for me."

"Wow!" said Peter again, then: "Will it be like that other summer when we went to that place in Greece?"

"Not quite," Father said, putting down his pen, "you see, Peter, we visited Greece so that I could continue the research for my books. Things can be a little more relaxed then, and that's why I don't mind if sometimes you and Sarah *have a go* at helping out on the site. This time in Rome, however, I shall not be in charge and I don't know if the authorities will let you on to their site. At any rate, you can go and tell Sarah all about it. Then, perhaps, I can finish off this part of the plan!"

Father picked his pen very purposefully and Peter took the hint. He went off to the kitchen in search of Sarah. It was while they were all rejoicing over the prospect of summer in Italy that the blow fell. Peter had found Sarah helping Mother to prepare supper. Mother had just suggested having spaghetti to help get everyone into the mood.

"And besides Rome," she said, "we might have time to visit other cities: Florence, Assisi, even Naples! We could go to the coast. I'm sure your Father won't mind if we are enjoying ourselves while he is busy. It will be wonderful."

The telephone rang. Mother picked up the receiver and almost immediately sat down on the stool that was next to her.

"Oh dear!" she said, then again, "Oh dear!"

After that she hummed and harr'd for some time and finished off with:

"Of course, I shall come at once. Tomorrow evening at the latest."

Peter and Sarah sat down on the kitchen chairs and observed the whole scene. It was obvious to them that something very serious had occurred.

When Mother put down the phone, she pursed her lips, wiped her eyes and walked purposefully away, out of the kitchen and down the hall to the study. Peter and Sarah heard the study door shut and waited for Father and Mother to sort out whatever it was.

When the study door opened again, it was Father who came out, looking very worried. Peter and Sarah had left the kitchen by this time and were sitting in the drawing room, which was next to the study.

"Mother is very upset," Father said, "Grandmother has the 'flu very badly and her neighbour, Mrs. Kandinsky, has helped to get her to hospital."

"Oh no!" cried Sarah, "that's awful!"

"Poor Gran," said Peter with feeling, for they were both very fond of their Grandmother, even though they did not see so much of her since their removal to Wales.

"Naturally Mother will go to her straight away and will stay until she is well enough to go home. She may even stay a bit longer than that. We will have to see."

"But who is going to look after us?" wailed Sarah and Peter.

"Oh I am sure Aunt Myf will come to the rescue," Father gave a wan half smile, "I will take you to school in the mornings and Aunt Myf or Uncle Tomos might collect you in the afternoon and hang on to you 'til I get back from work. Now then, I am going to telephone to Aunt Myf right this minute. Sarah, you hop upstairs and help Mother pack. Peter, back to the kitchen with you and carry on getting the supper out. I'll come and help you shortly." So saying Father went to the phone and Peter and Sarah flew to their posts.

The rest of the evening was a flurry of activity and the following morning saw the whole family up with the lark. Father took Mother to the station where many 'Goodbyes' were said, some of them tearful. Having waved Mother off on her long journey to London, Father drove Sarah and Peter to school and then went to work.

Later on that morning, during break time, Peter sought Sarah out and finally caught up with her behind the School Hall where she and some of her friends were playing skipping. When Peter came round the corner of the new building, Sarah bade her friends a hasty adieu and ran to meet him. She could see at once by his face that something momentous was afoot.

"It's time!" Peter announced solemnly, as he walked with Sarah to the Junior's Organic Garden project.

Beside the new flower and vegetable beds there was a seat Peter sat down and Sarah joined him.

"Time for what?" said Sarah, though with a sinking feeling, she thought she knew.

"Time to see Gwyn-ap-Nudd."

"How do you know that it's time?" asked Sarah.

"I just know, all right," replied Peter rather grouchily. "If you must know, I've had this funny feeling in the pit of my stomach ever since I woke up."

"Ah," said Sarah, interrupting, "indigestion!"

"Of course it isn't."

"Or you're missing Mum already, or upset about Gran."

"No, and no!" Peter replied emphatically.

He bit his lip, a habit he had when under stress.

"I *know* that we've just GOT to see Gwyn-ap-Nudd now, or as soon as possible."

"But HOW?" asked Sarah.

"I have thought up a most ingenious plan," Peter replied, and smiled his special secret smile.

"I see," said Sarah, but she did not really and unfortunately there was no time to talk about it any more, as the bell rang for the end of breaktime.

The children did not manage to meet each other again until Aunt Myf appeared at the school gates to collect them at three fifteen precisely. By that time Sarah was on tenterhooks and felt that if she did not hear Peter's plan very soon, she was going to burst!

When they arrived at Aunt Myf's house in Newport, Peter and Sarah went straight into the kitchen for tea, while Aunt Myf went straight to Catrin, who was yelling about something or another.

"Please dears, help yourselves, I've put plenty out."

And indeed she had. There were tomato sandwiches, egg sandwiches, crisps, a jelly, small iced cakes, lemonade and chocolate biscuits.

"Goodness knows when your Father will arrive from work," said Aunt Myf, as she planted a bottle teat firmly between Catrin's rosy lips, "so you'd better eat up."

When they felt that they had done justice to most of the tea, Sarah pulled Peter out of the kitchen door and into the garden. It was a bleak January afternoon; dull, and almost, but not quite, raining.

"I've simply GOT to know!" Sarah pleaded, "what is this plan you have cooked up?"

"Ah ha!"

Peter laughed and leaped away from her. Then he ran down to the bottom of the garden.

"Ooooh! You rotten tease!" shouted Sarah at him, as she ran round the opposite side in order to surprise him upon the other side of the privet hedge that divided flowers from vegetables.

"OK, all right, I give in!" panted Peter as Sarah caught him by the arm.

He went over to sit on the garden bench and Sarah followed.

"It was my friend Ben who gave me the idea."

"Come on, spill the beans, what idea?"

"Keep your hair on! I'm coming to it. Well, you see Ben told me that there's this Cyber Café in Haverfordwest. He often goes in there to surf the net while his parents go shopping."

"So?" Sarah said, unimpressed, "we have a computer at home."

"Yes, but Dad's always busy on it doing work. He is so awfully busy at the moment, isn't he? All the lectures that he has to do, his books, stuff for his students, not to mention the plan for the *dig* in Rome this summer."

"Yes, yes, but how does all this help get us to Arx Emain?"

"Well, you know how keen everyone is on technology, especially people at school... I think you and I might suddenly be very keen to have a look at this Cyber Café. It might help us with our homework!"

"I still don't see how... and I haven't got any homework that needs a computer."

"Silly girl! You don't need to have homework. Listen... Aunt Myf likes shopping in Haverfordwest, doesn't she? I don't think Dad will mind if we ask her to give us a lift down there in order to have a go on the internet. We'll get her to drop us off at the Cyber Café, then we'll tell her we don't know how long we are going to be and that we will take the bus back home!"

Sarah began to see a glimmer of light.

"Yes, yes!" she cried excitedly, "and if we take the bus back, we can stop off very near to Arx Emain..."

"Visit Gwyn-ap-Nudd and there you are!" Peter finished triumphantly.

Then he got up and bowed to a large, but imaginary audience. It began to rain properly. Peter did not care. He danced round the lawn with Sarah copying his movements. Then, finally, when they found themselves getting cold as well as wet, they ran into Aunt Myf's house, whooping for joy.

Aunt Myf gave them both a bath towel to dry off. They sat in front of the sitting room fire and did their homework very nicely until Dr. Jones arrived to collect his children at half past six.

"How have they been?" he asked.

"No trouble at all," said Aunt Myf, "and you are in nice time too! Look, here's my Tomos home already. Goodbye Peter and Sarah, I'll see you tomorrow, same time, same place. Until then be good and look after your Father. Bye, bye, everybody!" she waved them off.

"There's something up with those two," she thought. "I'll have to keep my eyes open and see what they get up to."

Then she forgot Peter and Sarah, as Catrin demanded her full attention once more and Detective Inspector Tomos Davies needed his supper.

It was a very bouncy Peter and Sarah who helped their Father get their meal that night. They telephoned Mother afterwards to enquire how things were going. Fortunately, Grandmother was just a little better, so they all celebrated by playing Sarah's Murder Mystery board game until it was time for bed.

As the two children went upstairs, Sarah whispered to Peter: "I'm sure your plan will work."

"Of course it will work!" Peter replied, emphatically, "and this Saturday we had better jolly well put it into action!"

So, over the course of the next few days a determined effort was made to persuade Father of their need to visit the Cyber Café.

"But there is a computer here," Dr. Jones protested at first.

"But Dad, you're always doing work on it and you won't let us use it to go on the net unless you are with us," said Peter persuasively.

"And," argued Sarah, "we've never been to a Cyber Café."

"My friend Ben often goes," Peter said, as coaxingly as he could and of course at last Father gave in.

"As long as it is no trouble for Aunt Myf," he said at length, "I mean, you can go just as long as she was going shopping in Haverfordwest anyway. You two are not to browbeat her into a journey that she does not want to do."

"No browbeating, we promise," Sarah said.

She knew that there would be no need for anything like that. Indeed, there was no problem at all in getting a lift from Aunt Myf; it was almost too easy.

"Of course you can come," she said, "I often go into town on a Saturday, you know I do. It's my little bit of relaxation. You can come any time you want, just let me know."

And that was that. It was all set!

The days dragged by, but at last it was Saturday morning. Peter and Sarah packed a rucksack each, filing them with edible provisions and other useful items. Sarah found a small box for the Ring of Concealment and buried it in the deepest pocket. "Perhaps, if I'm lucky, Anir will take the beastly thing back," she thought.

They made a good breakfast of boiled eggs, Cornflakes and lots of hot buttered toast, washing it all down with a pot of tea. As soon as Father was safe at work in the study, Peter and Sarah got their heavy jackets, picked up the rucksacks and left the house. There was plenty of time before they were due to meet Aunt Myf at the main road, so they strolled up the drive at a leisurely pace. It was a beautiful morning, bright, sunny and clear. There was just a touch of hoar frost upon the grass, trees and bushes. Everything seemed to sparkle.

"I wonder what Gwyn-ap-Nudd really wants with us," said Sarah. Now that the meeting was about to happen, they both began to think of what they might be in for!

"Oh, I expect he wants a few more monsters dispatched," Peter replied airily, "no trouble, no problem! Peter and Sarah's

ACME Monster Control Company, Inc. Get your monsters dealt with here!"

"Oh silly boy," laughed Sarah, and they continued on up the drive in a merry mood, laughing and giggling all the way.

"You two seem in a good temper today," said Aunt Myf, when they met her on the main road. "Jump in dears, just throw the rucksacks in the back will you and we'll be off."

So saying she put the car radio on and they all had a sing song right down to Haverfordwest.

When they arrived, Aunt Myf said that she was going to park at the big supermarket.

"I'm going to take advantage of the fact that Uncle Tomos is looking after Catrin this morning. If you are finished before me, meet me in the car park at twelve. I shall leave at quarter past at the latest. If you are not there on the dot, I shall assume that you are getting the bus back."

"Right!" said Peter, patting the pocket in his rucksack which held the bus timetable.

"Bye then Peter, Sarah; be good and don't do anything I wouldn't do. When do you have to be home?"

"By tea time," Sarah replied and gave Aunt Myf her most innocent smile.

"Very well then! Just see to it that you are," Aunt Myf then gave the pair of them an extra big wink that meant:

"I know you're up to something!"

Then she departed for the supermarket.

"She winked," said Sarah, "do you think she suspects anything?"

"I don't know Sis, but we had better shift ourselves and get on with our plan. We haven't got that much time."

Peter began to walk away in a hurry towards the bus depot. On the way, they happened to pass the Cyber Café. By a stroke of luck they saw that Ben was in there already. Peter and Sarah called in to say *hello* and stayed there as long as they dared. They had a look at a web site about volcanoes, which was one of Ben's odder hobbies, expressed the appropriate amount of interest, then left as soon as it felt proper to do so.

"That's good!" said Peter, "Now we have an alibi."

"Really, brother mine, you sound as if we were going to rob a bank."

Peter decided to make no further remark and the two of them plodded off to find the right bus.

As they came to the depot, Peter noticed that there was a bus already in with its sign up for Fishguard.

"That'll do, Sarah, jump on."

Sarah did as she was bid. She could not decide whether she was feeling excited or nervous. Peter squeezed her hand. For all his brave words he knew that HE felt nervous. They had not been to the Elves at Arx Emain for well over a year. While they were with them on their last sojourn in the underground realm, somehow Peter and Sarah had become used to them and their ways... but now?

The bus had not gone far, when familiar landmarks told the children that it was almost time to ring the bell to get off. The Cleddau River began to be on their right instead of on the left. They passed a small village.

"There ought to be a request stop coming up in a minute," said Sarah rather uncertainly.

As so much time had passed since their last visit to Arx Emain she had started to doubt her memories of how she had come there. It was not an easy place to find and Sarah knew that there was more than one entrance. Would they be able to find their way to the front door? Peter pressed the bell for the bus to stop. The bus obediently drew to a halt, Peter and Sarah thanked the driver and got off. Peter picked up his rucksack and heaved it on to his back.

"I do apologise," he said, "I think I pressed the bell too early. I am sure that we are one stop short, we should have gone on a little further to the north."

"Never mind," said Sarah, as she adjusted the straps on her rucksack, "we can walk a bit. After all, we've done it before and usually when something or someone was after us!"

"True, Sis," replied her brother, "come on then, it can't take us that long to find the front door, or rather we had better not take too long, otherwise we shall be late getting home."

"Yes, and then we'll be in trouble and THEY won't let us out on our own ever again," Sarah said and plunged off northwards into the scrub with Peter following.

They passed through a small wood and fortunately found a public footpath, which seemed to be going vaguely in the right direction. Then the going became rougher. Scrub and rough grasses gave way to gorse and brambles. To their left the ground rose upwards in a gentle slope.

"Shouldn't we be turning more to the left?" asked Sarah, after half an hour's steady plodding during which Peter had insisted upon taking over the leadership!

"Not yet," Peter said firmly, "I'm sure that we still have to go north more than we are."

He said this with an air of overwhelming confidence. However, after over a year away from the Elves, he felt a twinge of uncertainty. Did he, could he remember where the doors into Arx Emain were exactly? Peter groaned inwardly. He had begun to realise that actually, really, truly neither of them were absolutely certain which way to go. After going on a few more steps, Peter suggested that they have something to eat from the rucksacks. This was in order to give himself time to think. Sarah agreed willingly. There were some rocks nearby which they used as seats while they took a couple of swigs each from the lemonade bottle and ate some of their sandwiches. As soon as she had finished, Sarah jumped up and picked up her rucksack.

"I'm ready," she said, "Where to now?"

"Well..." Peter said, very slowly, as if considering their next move.

Sarah cut him short.

"I'm leading from here," she said firmly, and went forwards quickly to where there seemed to be some ancient earthworks. Peter followed her, glad that Sarah seemed to know where she was going. In fact Sarah thought she did know the way. They passed the earthworks and some very large rocks. Shortly afterwards, the path they had been following gave out. They could both see that down in a dip below them there was a stream.

"What's this?" asked Peter. "I don't remember this stream at all. Have we come too far north now?"

"I think that I might remember," Sarah said, "just give me a minute will you!"

She looked worried and started to pace up and down beside the stream. At last she said:

"I think we ought to cross the stream. I'm sure that I can see trees in the distance."

"I shall trust in your superior knowledge," Peter said dryly, with a wry smile, "after all, you have been *in and out* of Arx Emain much more than I have."

"That's true Peter, but I always came from another direction, north, east, west but never from the south."

"North or south, we'd better hurry up and decide which way to go, it's midday already!

"Ooooh! What to do, what to do?"

Sarah began to wring her hands, as she always did when feeling under pressure.

"We have come so far, and now it looks as if we'll have to go back without seeing the Elves at all!"

"We could try going to the top of the hill over there and then we might see what's what."

"No, I think it will be better if we go towards those trees."

They wasted five more precious minutes arguing as to whether it would be better to view the whole scene from the hill top, or to go for the trees! Then Sarah lost her patience and her temper.

"It's me Ederyn wanted, it's me," she yelled at Peter, "because it's *my* ring that they want, I'm going this way!" and she sped off down the bank and towards the stream.

As she ran, she looked about wildly for somewhere to cross the dark, swirling, bubbling waters. Thank goodness, yes, there was a nice little bridge. Sarah ran over and followed the footpath that led off to the left. Peter was close behind her, in hot pursuit. Sarah could hear his footsteps clatter over the bridge behind her.

On and on she ran, as if she were in training for the Olympics. Past some buildings that might have been a farm, but she did not stop to look, and on and on. Peter was beginning to catch her up. Sarah could feel that he was close behind, his breathing was heavy: 'Huh, Huh'. Sarah began to catch her breath also, but she could see that she was nearly there now. On and on she ran, pushing herself to the very limit.

"Yes, yes! I'm under the trees at last, at last!"

Sarah dropped down on to her hands and knees and about half a minute later, Peter did the same. Neither of them could speak for quite a while.

They put all their energies into breathing. At length, after a few minutes, the two children began to feel like continuing the search for the elusive kingdom of the Elves. Peter got up from the ground. He took off his rucksack to adjust the straps again. Turning to face Sarah, he was just about to say:

"I told you so, there's no-one here!" when Sarah pointed over his shoulder.

She mouthed silently:

"LOOK!"

Peter turned round slowly.

Peering at them from behind one of larger trees was a very strange personage. As far as they could tell, this person was not one of the Elves, not one that they had ever met, anyway. Who could it be, and why was he here in the wood when they were half expecting to meet Anir The Guardian, or Ederyn?

CHAPTER THREE

Merlin

Peter and Sarah stared at the personage who continued to peer at them from behind the tree. It seemed like hours, but must only have been a few minutes. Eventually, Sarah thought that they might appear rude if introductions were not made shortly! She got up from the ground and walked forward, her hand outstretched.

"Hello, how do you do? I'm Sarah and this is my brother Peter."

The personage came out from behind the tree, smiling broadly. He took Sarah's hand and shook it warmly.

"I am Merlin," he said, "and I have been waiting for you."

"Waiting for us?" gasped Sarah.

"Are you, by any chance, *THE* Merlin?" said Peter.

He just could not help himself.

"I am, as far as I know, the *only* Merlin, now or then or to be!" returned Merlin, "and I have been waiting here for you for quite some time. The last three days, off and on, to be precise. You see, *they* said that you were coming, but they were not quite sure when... Soon! he said. It will be very soon, we have sent them many, many thought messages."

"He?" asked Peter.

"Gwyn-ap-Nudd, of course," Merlin smiled. "You will need a good explanation for all your troubles, I can tell, and the Lord Gwyn is waiting and longing to give it to you. We must hurry."

"You're right," said Peter, trying to conceal his surprise, "we don't have much time; less than three hours before we must be home again."

Merlin smiled benevolently at the two children. Sarah was fascinated by him. Neither she nor Peter could help staring at him. Merlin was not at all what they expected and they had difficulty in believing that this was King Arthur's famous magician friend. He looked so ordinary, and much too young. He looked to be about the same age as their own Father and therefore could hardly expect to be taken too seriously!

Then there were his clothes. They were certainly unusual, but not exactly what one supposed to be the uniform of a wizard. There was no pointed hat, in fact no hat at all. He had no beard and no purple cape with stars and moons on it. He wore a simple wool tunic, a dull mustard in colour, over some kind of linen undergarment, with a battered and tattered cloak of an indistinct bluey, purpley shade over the top. He did however carry a staff. Some recompense for not having a wand, Sarah thought.

"Very well!" said Merlin, "Very well indeed! And now door, show yourself."

Sarah and Peter gasped again as Merlin pointed the long staff, upon which he had been leaning all this while, at a face of rock which suddenly appeared before them.

"We haven't moved," thought Peter, "But we are definitely somewhere else."

"When did we leave the trees behind?" thought Sarah, "Perhaps we are in a dream."

The rocks made a very curious scraping noise and parted obediently. Merlin poked them with his staff.

"As if he were jabbing someone in the stomach," Peter whispered under his breath.

When there was enough of a doorway, Merlin encouraged the two astonished children to pass through it into a tunnel. This was a stone lined tunnel, carved upon either side with all kinds of leaves. Small lamps lit the way every now and again. In fact it was just like all the corridors and tunnels within…

"Arx Emain!" Sarah and Peter cried out at once.

"Good old Merlin, you have found what we were looking for," said Peter.

"Yes, quite! Of course, and what did you expect? I would not be waiting for you out in the wild without the back door to hand, as it were. But come along and do hurry up. This tunnel is quite a long one and Gwyn does not like to be kept waiting. As a matter of fact," he added as an afterthought, "neither do I. For your information, Peter and Sarah, Arx Emain was under your feet all the time!"

With this last remark, Merlin sped off down the tunnel.

"Like greased lightening," Sarah thought, "I bet he's much fitter than either of our parents, or me! I can hardly keep up with him."

The two children tried to follow their new acquaintance, as best they could after their mammoth run just moments before. Fifteen to twenty minutes later, Peter and Sarah recognised exactly where they were.

"Stay here!" commanded Merlin from over his shoulder, as he disappeared round the corner. Peter and Sarah waited where they were in a state of great excitement.

"We're almost at the Great Hall," said Peter, his voice trembling just a little.

"Yes, I know, but I didn't see where we were until about two turns ago."

"Gwyn must be waiting in the Hall and Merlin has gone to announce us."

"Why don't we just go straight in, it's only a little way round the corner. I'm sure the Elves won't mind," said Sarah.

She was impatient to get on with the job, now that they were actually inside the Elves' domain.

"They might think that a bit rude," Peter was uncertain, "but we might give it a try. I'm sure that they know that we are in a hurry."

They took two paces forward. Then, from around the corner where Merlin had disappeared moments before, came the familiar figure of an old friend:

"Anir!" cried Peter and Sarah at once, "we thought we might never see you again."

Anir came quickly forward to greet them, his arms outstretched in welcome:

"This is good," he said, as both gave him a bear hug, "it is good that we meet once again, excellent in fact!"

"We did miss you," said Sarah as they followed Anir down the passageway to the Great Hall.

"Really?" Anir said quizzically.

One of his eyebrows shot up and he stared hard at them both. Peter blushed. A habit he had from his earliest infancy. Anir gave him the most piercing of gazes.

"I thought your family had been FAR too busy recently to think about Elves and their friends!"

He said this in a way that was not unfriendly, it was a matter of fact. Indeed, the family had been very busy over the last year and a half.

"It seems we need your assistance once more. That is, if you agree to what Gwyn-ap-Nudd has in mind. Come along quickly now," said Anir, as they passed through the entrance of the Great Hall which was full of the residents of Arx Emain.

They saw Gwyn himself, sitting enthroned upon the dais and surrounded by the senior members of the Elf Kingdom, some of whom Peter and Sarah had got to know quite well. Ederyn was present, Aneryn and Morvith the Healer also. All three had been very helpful to the children during their last escapade.

"Welcome my friends, welcome once again to Arx Emain," said Lord Gwyn, smiling and beckoning them forwards to the foot of the dais.

They stood there before all, feeling really rather embarrassed. The assembled company had obviously just finished their midday meal and Peter and Sarah felt all eyes upon them. Peter went bright red again. Merlin was standing to one side of Gwyn-ap-Nudd looking anxious.

"Now, I am sure you would like to know why you have been summoned," the Lord Gwyn said to them solemnly.

"Yes please," answered Peter and Sarah together.

"Sarah, you *have* brought The Ring, have you not?" Gwyn asked.

"Yes, just a minute," she replied, holding up her rucksack.

She put the sack down on the floor and fumbled inside for the container that held the ring. Quickly she took the ring out and placed it on her right ring finger.

"Here it is," she said, and pointed to the jewel, which gleamed and sparkled in the light of the many candles and lamps around the Hall.

"Very good," said Gwyn, "now, you have already met Merlin who has brought you here today, have you not?"

This was a rhetorical question for he then went on to say:

"It is he who needs our help and yours in a most daring expedition. Will you hear what he has to say?"

Peter and Sarah willingly agreed. Two stools were brought for them to sit on. They placed their rucksacks on the floor nearby and all opened their ears to listen to what Merlin had to say.

"I have come through time, via the land of the Summer Stars, to see what help could be given us. By US, I mean Us Britons, and all who are faithful to Our Lord and Emperor, Arthur."

" WOW!" Peter could not help exclaiming out loud.

Was it not every boy's dream to meet someone from the magic realm of Camelot, if not King Arthur himself?

"Arthur is but young as yet," Merlin continued, "it is only a few years since he pulled the sword out of the stone, pacified the British tribal chiefs and established his reign. However, although we have been granted an interval of peace, and I am well aware," Merlin looked sharply at the Lord Gwyn-ap-Nudd as he said this, "that it will be but a short interval. Young Arthur feels that he must put his Imperium over Britannia, and Little Britannia Over the Sea, entirely beyond the question of any doubt. So of course, when the Roman Proconsul arrived to demand that we pay tribute to Rome once more..."

"Rome?" gasped Sarah.

"Rome!" exclaimed Peter, for now they were both completely confused and utterly mystified.

When Merlin had begun to speak of King Arthur, visions of mediaeval ladies in pointed hats with their knights in shining armour began to ride about in Sarah's head. Camelot, Sir Lancelot and the Round Table all shimmered in a magical haze. All these images promptly disappeared in a puff of smoke.

Peter was thinking:

"Rome, Ancient Rome! Now I know why Merlin looks so odd to us. Look at him, he is holding his cloak so that it drapes like a toga. I am sure I have seen pictures of Julius Caesar looking just like that!"

"Yes Rome!" replied Merlin. "Although many of our people are by this time almost more Roman than those who live in that city, it has been many, many years since we paid tribute. Indeed, we have not paid the Roman authorities any taxes or tribute, from the time that the Roman High-ups departed for Rome when the Empire began to be threatened by barbarians.

Now we Britons have had our troubles too. Invaders from the North Lands have pressed our peoples badly. To tell the truth, our leaders have often sent to Rome for help against our common enemies, but recently no help has been forthcoming. Can you see why Arthur is angry with Rome? All we Britons are very, very angry!"

Peter nudged Sarah:

"I can see why they are angry. I would be too," he whispered.

Merlin cleared his throat:

"Well now, Hem, Hem! My opinion is that the present Emperor of the once proud and glorious Roman Empire," Merlin looked his most scornful as he said this, "that is, Odovacer, who is a usurper, needs monies urgently. I fancy the tribute is required in order to fight off the armies of the Emperor in the East. Zeno has no love for upstarts and usurpers like Odovacer. It cannot be for battles with barbarians, *they* all seem to be with us in Britannia! As our chiefs wrote to Aetius years ago, when he was Consul for the third time:

"The barbarians drive us to the sea; the sea throws us back on the barbarians. Thus, two modes of death await us, we can either be slain or drowned!"

Thus have the Britons made known their groans to the Roman authorities for years uncountable and the Romans send us no help. Pah!"

Merlin made as if to spit upon the guilty, but un-present Romans.

"When we return from this campaign, the Lord Arthur will be strong enough, I hope, to give the Saxons a convincingly final defeat! Then we Britons will have peace and plenty once more, just as it was under the best of the Caesars."

Gwyn-ap-Nudd nodded sympathetically.

"You have to understand, Peter and Sarah, that by the time the high-and-mighty ones went back to Rome in 410, THEY were the *few*. The Romans who were left behind stayed because they were *Roman Britons*. Many of the legionaries who came to conquer these Islands married British women and also, of course, there were the free people of these Islands who became Roman citizens and took on everything that the Romans had to offer. Much of it was very good. I know, I was there!"

Sarah jumped in her seat, for she had just been thinking: how does *he* know all that? Forgetting that being an Elf, Gwyn had seen many ages come and go.

Gwyn nodded his head, as if in answer to Sarah's unspoken thought.

"Yes, the Romans were a civilising influence here for nearly five hundred years."

Gwyn forbore to say that unfortunately, as even Peter and Sarah knew well, in the end the Saxons had indeed prevailed, thus paving the way for the rise of the English. Gwyn himself had not been overly sympathetic to the Saxon rulers, although he knew that even Alfred the Great had once dwelt in Rome and looked back to the Eternal City for inspiration.

"Gosh!" Sarah said, "that's like us looking back to the time of Queen Elizabeth the first! That IS a long time for the Romans to be around. I never thought of it like that before."

"But why do you need us?" Peter asked.

"Merlin needs the Ring that Anir gave to Sarah, the Ring of Concealment! We thought that possibly one of you... *Peter perhaps?* might like the honour of using it in the service of The Emperor Arthur," replied Gwyn.

Questions flooded into Peter's brain, the main one being, how was one transported back into the decline and fall of the Roman Empire? Gwyn-ap-Nudd's answer came swiftly:

"Merlin wishes to make use of the power of the Gardar Stone to transport the Ring and one or other, or both of your good selves perhaps, to where Lord Arthur and his armies lie. They are far in time and far abroad, hoping shortly to engage in battle with the wretched Roman representative."

"He is not Roman, actually," Merlin said bitterly, "he is an Iberian."

"That means he's Spanish," Peter whispered in Sarah's ear.

"As I was saying," Gwyn went on, "I believe that The Lord Arthur has refused, finally and most definitely, to pay this tribute. So, before the Emperor's army comes to take it by force, he has decided to teach this upstart and his Proconsul a lesson. That is assuming that the Eastern Emperor Zeno, or his protégé Theodoric..."

Merlin nodded his confirmation.

"do not get to Odovacer first!"

"That is roughly correct," agreed Merlin, "our spies tell us that Zeno's associate, Theodoric, is already on his way to Rome.

Arthur remains undecided at the moment as to whether he should join forces with him or not, two armies being greater than one. He may join up with him later on.

First things first! I need to find a small, discreet and preferably invisible spy for Arthur. We shall come to a point very shortly when we need some vital information, so that our forces can set up the ultimate battle plan. I have been thinking of the rings of concealment for some time. I know where one of them is, but the Lady Fair who has it will not give it up to me, not for all my best wheedling! There are others... whose whereabouts I do not know and cannot find out, and there is the oldest one of them all, the fabled Ring of Gyges."

Peter and Sarah looked vacantly at Merlin. They had not heard of the name of Gyges in any tale, however ancient. The Lord Gwyn gazed on their wonderment and came to the rescue.

"The Ring of Gyges," Gwyn began, "The Ring of Gyges was brought to Britain by strangers who came to join your ancient ancestors here; I forget how many millennia ago, one or two, at least, perhaps three, I cannot now remember exactly. They came from the East and gained possession of the Ring during their long, tedious and meandering journeys here from Troy. Legend has it that they took it by force from a thief. Before he died of his wounds, he told this story:

He had once been a slave in the court of the King of Lydia. The King had been very disturbed in his ways and became more so as time ran on. People at court wondered if he were not mad. The slave kept watch on him and discovered at length the secret of the Ring and also how he came by it. To his surprise the King in his ramblings disclosed that he also once had lowly beginnings, having been a shepherd in the service of the former King. One day, an earthquake had revealed an opening into a cave. Being of a curious nature, Gyges, for that was his name, entered the cave. Inside was a body, naked except for a ring. Thinking to enrich himself, Gyges stole the ring and left the cave directly. Passing among his fellow shepherds, Gyges soon discovered that if he turned the jewel in a certain way he became invisible. It was all a wonderful game, a huge joke to begin with. Then Gyges began to use the ring unwisely and with malice in his heart. Eventually he used it to kill the King, marry the Queen and take over the kingdom. I believe he was a very strong and successful ruler of Lydia after that and was famous for joining forces with the Egyptian Pharaoh to beat off the Babylonians."

"And I heard he was a slimy, untrustworthy customer, always making alliances anywhere he could and then reneging on them," rejoined Merlin.

"Be that as it may," said the Lord Gwyn, "The Ring of Gyges was stolen from the King in its turn by this slave, who died rather than give it up. Then, it was given to one of the British Chieftains, a descendant of Auvandil himself, as a wedding gift on his marriage to the Princess of the strangers from Troy, the East, or wherever it was they came from.

When his time came and he died, all the British Chieftains came in delegation and brought the Ring to the Elves. We decided it must be used only for the good of Britain, as it seemed to have had such a bad history. Ederyn, myself and the Council could see that it was something very powerful, precious and special. It was given to **The Guardian** then, as only he was deemed to be worthy of keeping it through the *many tests* that go with that office and **the Apprenticeship to it**..."

The Lord Gwyn said this last sentence very loudly, as if to gain the attention of any whose attention had wandered!

Peter suddenly knew that Gwyn was looking right at him, through him, into his very soul almost. He felt that the Elf Lord was searching him, testing him, asking him something. What was it and why? It brought his heart up into his mouth up with a jolt.

While Gwyn had been speaking, Peter had been day dreaming about being one of the old chieftains; someone like the great Auvandil himself. Ever since the Elves' war with Arddu, Peter had often fancied himself as a warrior; fighting the evil enemy, whoever that might be, with shield and sword. Images of battles played in his mind, in which he was naturally always the victor! Perhaps one wonderful, marvellous day he would be able to fight for the Elves like Anir did... perhaps he might even ask Anir to help him learn how to do so... perhaps, perhaps...

Then the Lord Gwyn's probing had broken into his private reverie. Peter realised that Gwyn knew *all* that he was thinking. He felt extremely embarrassed and blushed as crimson as the tunic Ederyn was wearing. Something like an alarm bell rang in his brain. He knew his deepest, darkest secrets were laid bare before the Elf King. What *did* Gwyn want of him, Peter began to ask himself, but for the present, he did not have time to consider or reflect upon an answer.

The Elf king went on with his story as if nothing out of the ordinary had passed between them:

"Sometimes even yet, Anir, our present Guardian has the need to be invisible; which we Elves naturally have of right. After that time, The Guardians always kept the Ring safely hidden here at Arx Emain and handed it down to each of their successors through the ages. Thus and so, here it has stayed until recently," Gwyn smiled at Sarah:

"Really, it is and should be, always in the keeping of The Guardian and ONLY The Guardian; though Anir has let you borrow it for the moment with our permission."

Peter wondered why they had left the treasure with Sarah for so long. Then he asked:

"But why couldn't Merlin ask you for the Ring in Roman times?" he asked suddenly.

"Because Gwyn back in the Roman times does not have the Ring of Gyges. The Guardian of the time has it and he is away on some very important business that cannot be disturbed. Gwyn says we cannot get it then. Perhaps the Guardian needs it himself. Anyway in my time, after the Roman authorities had gone completely, the Elves shut themselves up in their palaces and left mankind to fight their own battles, in the main."

Merlin frowned furiously and clicked his tongue impatiently.

"That is not entirely true," Gwyn broke in, "one of my own kinsmen joined Arthur's great adventure in Gaul and he was killed. Also, do not forget, Merlin, that I was one who was foremost in the hunting of the great boar."

"Hmm, yes, EVENTUALLY!" said Merlin, insinuating that not a little persuasion had been required!

"But how is it," insisted Peter, "that you are able to get help in the future, won't it change what goes on in the past?"

"Not at all," Merlin smiled, "why, I am engaged upon the *Past, Present and Future Business* all the time. Now little people, will you not tell me what you would like to do? Will you come with Merlin? You will at least lend me the Ring, I am sure of that."

Sarah looked at the Ring. She knew it really belonged to Anir? But was it *so* important? She knew it must be if the Elves said so, but she could hardly believe it. It did not look *that* special. In her own heart she was still not awfully sure that she wanted to go, nor did she want to let Peter go either. It all sounded rather too scary. Then she took a long look right around the Great Hall and the bright company of Elves seated round the tables. They were all dressed most elegantly in the brightest colours, dazzling crimsons and heavenly blues. Everyone seemed to be waiting for her to speak. Even Peter was looking at her expectantly. He would definitely want to go, Sarah knew that much! At length she said in a very small voice:

" Could Peter and I talk it over, just for a few minutes, please?"

"But of course," replied the Lord Gwyn, getting up from his throne, "you may go to the Room of the Gardar Stone if you wish," and he waved them away.

Peter and Sarah got up from the stools and picked up the rucksacks. They bowed solemnly to Gwyn and to Merlin. The occasion seemed to demand some kind of obeisance. Then they walked with as much dignity as they could muster and as quickly as they dared, out of the Hall. The noise of many chattering voices rose like an ocean wave behind them, then fell silent as the two children ran down the corridor and into the room of the Stone of Gardar.

Sarah and Peter passed through the huge wooden doors, which were carved from top to bottom with every kind of beast, real and mythological. Unicorns stood next to lions and dragons next to squirrels and butterflies. Both of them felt the atmosphere of the room gather them into itself. It was such a peaceful place. Within its niche the Stone of Gardar glowed with a pale green light, revealing the stone pillars round the room and the dais and throne of Gwyn-ap-Nudd. Everywhere gleamed gold, the light of pure Welsh gold. Sarah dropped her rucksack on the floor. Peter followed suit and once more they found themselves sitting on the dais and wondering what on earth, or under it, to do next!

"We've simply got to go, haven't we," began Peter excitedly.

"Well, I'm none too sure," Sarah replied, desperately searching for an excuse not to take part in the mad sounding mission, "Sounds to me like cheating."

"What does?"

"Using the Ring of Concealment to beat this Roman guy."

"Whose side are you on!" Peter retorted, angrily.

"The right side, King Arthur's side of course, silly! I'm sure that Merlin and Arthur are quite right not to pay the tribute. I just wonder if invisible spies are perhaps *not quite cricket*."

"Not quite cricket!" Peter repeated incredulously, "not quite cricket! Really Sarah, I wonder about you sometimes. Arthur is fighting a war, a war that must be won..."

His voice lowered:

"Yes, that's it, Arthur has to win this war, or the course of history will be changed."

"Are you sure of that, Peter? After all, walloping Romans isn't in any of the books that I've read about King Arthur."

"No, nor I, but perhaps we have been reading the wrong books."

Peter frowned and was silent for a moment. Sarah waited, for she knew that he was thinking. Suddenly, Peter smiled.

"I've got it!" he said.

"What?"

"Why King Arthur isn't in the right time in all our books."

"What do you mean? What are you wittering on about Peter?"

"The reason why Arthur isn't written about at all until so much later and why they put him in the wrong time entirely!"

"Why then?"

"Well, Sarah," said Peter, looking at her very seriously, "if *you* were a Saxon Monk, writing the history of Saxon kings... would you write about Arthur and sing the praises of their WORST enemy? No, I think not! You probably wouldn't even mention him. In fact, you probably wouldn't be allowed to mention him! You'd probably get your head cut off if you did. I bet that's what happened... and it went on like that for hundreds of years, until the Saxon kings were gone and the Vikings too.

Then the stories about Arthur seeped back into England from the Britons in France who, with the Britons here in the furthest west, had kept his memory alive. The French troubadours must have got hold of the old stories and sung them in the courts of the Normans. Only then would it have been safe to praise the name of Arthur again. Yeah, I bet that's just what happened. The

Normans would have enjoyed a link to Arthur, *Scourge of the Saxons*! They would want to be associated with Arthur as that would strengthen their claim to the British Kingdom; especially as they were not Britons or Bretons at all, but originally Norsemen! I wonder when the stories reappear? I must check that out when we get home."

"Maybe," said Sarah, nodding her head, "it's a nice theory, but it doesn't change my opinion, which is: that we should give the jolly old Ring to jolly old Merlin, or back to Anir perhaps and let him get on with it!"

"Well, suppose, just suppose," Peter said passionately, sounding extremely annoyed, "that maybe, just maybe, I might like to go and meet King Arthur! And I can tell you right now, Sis, that I would!"

"Oh, come on, Bro. How can you, we, go and do that? It would take days, even months perhaps. It would be much worse than last time and probably more dangerous. I can't see how you can consider it, what with Gran so ill and Mum away."

The mention of Mother brought Peter back to reality.

"Sorry, Sis, but it would be rather fine, wouldn't it," he begged, "to meet King Arthur."

He said this last rather wistfully, pleading at Sarah with his eyes. Sarah was not to be put off.

"I'm not going to be an invisible spy for anyone."

"Well nobody said it had to be *you*, in fact, I think that Gwyn was telling us just now that it ought to be *me*!"

Peter was on the attack again. Sarah was just thinking up something really biting to round off her argument, when Anir suddenly came into the Golden Room.

"Hello," he said, "come to a decision have you?"

"No," said Peter at once.

"Yes," said Sarah, a millisecond later, "I am afraid, Anir, that we will have to say *no,* to Mr. Merlin's offer of a visit to King

Arthur but he can have the Ring. Why don't you take it now, after all Anir, it is yours."

"If it belongs to anyone... and I can tell you now, I have used it many times in my work as Guardian. However, I have not used it much these last few years, hardly at all in fact. I leave it with Gwyn more often than not. It is not necessary for me to have it at present, that is why I loaned it to you Sarah. I knew that it would be in safe hands, for you are brave and innocent in heart and mind."

Sarah smiled at the compliment. Anir watched as Peter frowned, he could imagine what the boy was thinking. He and Gwyn had both had their eyes on him for some time.

"Your turn will come Peter... and perhaps sooner than you think! Keep the Ring for now between the both of you and take your time to decide what to do. Your choice must be a free and clear one. Come both of you, we must return to the Great Hall. You do not have time for a long visit today and Merlin would like some kind of answer, even if it is only half an answer."

Peter and Sarah grabbed their rucksacks and ran out of the Golden Room of the Stone with Anir following them. When they entered the Great Hall, they found that nearly all the Elves had left. Those who were left upon the dais were: Gwyn, Ederyn, Merlin and Aneryn. Echel, the Master Armourer of the Elves, was there also; standing just to one side of Ederyn.

"I'm glad that Aneryn is there," thought Sarah, "I wonder if we can have some time to talk with her?"

But there was no time to wonder more because she and Peter had arrived at the foot of the dais and were being inspected by those upon the top of it.

"So, you were unable to decide," said Gwyn, looking deep into Sarah's eyes, "to stay, or to go... to take part, or not, these are difficult questions."

"Yes, er well, perhaps," Sarah muttered, feeling confused.

"I wish you'd make your mind up!" Peter hissed, as he gave her a hard dig in the ribs, "I want to go."

"Lord Gwyn, I really don't know what to do," said Sarah, "Merlin can have the Ring, of course he can, though I don't want to be a spy and wear it myself. Just the same, I would quite like to meet King Arthur, and I know Peter would too."

Peter blushed a very nice beetroot colour. It was true! Almost more than anything else right now, he wanted to see the legendary King. Besides, the thought of actually joining in one of King (or was it Emperor) Arthur's adventures, even if it did not appear in any of the usual books, was irresistible!

"But," Sarah continued, "how long would it take to get there and how long to come back? How much time would we have to spend there, and really, what I am trying to say is; how can we go without worrying our family?"

Merlin stepped forwards immediately to explain:

"My dear Sarah I, and all who support The Lord Arthur's worthy cause, thank you for your most generous offer of the Ring. Within the rules of magic, these things have to be given up willingly! If you really do want to come back with me and meet the Emperor, why certainly you may! It is most simple, I assure you."

Merlin looked sideways at Gwyn, as if seeking approval for what he was about to say. Gwyn nodded twice and Merlin continued with his explanation.

"How do you think I arrived here? Eh, Eh! I came through the power of the Gardar Stone of course."

Merlin almost jumped up and down with the excitement of it. "I had discussed the power of the Stone with Gwyn many, many years before. He had told me about it because the Elves had lost it and wanted me to help them find it once again. We had all wandered up and down the Prescelly Mountains; up and down, up and down. The Elves had not found it, nor I, nor the

Guardian. Then I required the Ring of Concealment in a hurry. How to come by it?"

"Why don't you look for the Stone in St. David's, where I found it?" Peter asked, interrupting the Wizard in full flow.

Gwyn answered him:

"Because my dear Peter, in Merlin's day, for some reason it is not yet there yet. Continue I pray, Merlin please."

"Where was I? Oh yes, I had the most splendid idea. You see, the power of the true magician lies in pure illusion."

Here Merlin put his right hand behind his back and brought out a beautiful bunch of snowdrops and gave it to Sarah.

"Wow, gosh!" gasped Sarah, as she took the flowers.

"Cool!" said Peter, as the flowers turned themselves into butterflies and fluttered about his head.

"Perhaps, I thought, somewhere in the future the Stone is found. If I could only *feel* the power of it, I might join my power to that power. Thus and so; I returned to that dark place, Foel Drygarn. It is deserted again. Any who were living there when the Romans came, had fled long ago. Now most people feel that there is no point returning there, unless they seek The Power. I made my enquiries and when I had discovered the right time and the right words, I made my preparations."

"What did you do?" Peter interrupted again. Merlin rewarded him with the broadest of grins.

"I managed to reproduce the Way of Light that leads to the Summer Stars and out again. For an instant I stood before those Bright Beings who hold almost the chiefest powers. I told them of my plight and that I needed the Stone of Gardar to get the Ring. Then in another instant I found myself in the Golden Room of the Stone. Quite an achievement, don't you think?"

Gwyn-ap-Nudd laughed out loud, stamped his foot and thumped the arm of the throne with his fist.

"Ha!" he said, and "Ha!" again. "Merlin is being far too modest my friends. This is not the first time he has attempted such a thing and succeeded. He is a very powerful magician indeed! But he likes people to think that he is the sort that entertains at court with the jester, pulling rabbits out of hats. Watch him carefully, Peter and Sarah, you will see him do much more than that. My heart tells me too that you will see him at work many times and that you *will* go to the camp of the Emperor."

"But how long will we have to be there?" Sarah persisted.

"As far as time goes, your time that is, you might be there and back in the twinkling of an eye. In fact, I doubt if any in our camp have missed me for an hour, yet I have been here three days at least."

"Well," said Peter, "we know that the Stone works in our time, we have seen it work. It worked on Mum and Dad, that time. What we don't know is, if it works properly in your time. I think Sarah needs just a little more time to think about it all."

Kind brother that he was, he said this in an attempt to allay Sarah's fears.

"Yes," Sarah added, "we don't want to get stuck in Hyperspace."

"Very well Peter," said Merlin, "you may have a week to think it all over. After that I shall take the Ring of Concealment and not trouble you further. Thereafter it shall be returned to the Guardian, who may accompany me himself, if he wishes."

Merlin bowed to Anir, who made a deep bow in return.

"I most certainly and quite definitely, am persuaded to come with you," smiled The Guardian.

He could not resist the thought of meeting King Arthur either!

Merlin continued:

"When you return, I will prove to you that you will be able to come and go as easily as you do on all your strange modern modes of transport."

"How is that?" asked Sarah.

"I shall return to camp. Then, when you come next week, I promise that I will bring you something that belongs to Arthur."

He bowed then to Sarah and then to Peter, thus completing his part of the discussion.

"One week at the most," said Gwyn firmly, giving Peter a very odd look, "and then we shall expect your speedy return. Now you must leave us. You must not be late home."

Aneryn came down from the dais and Ederyn also. Peter and Sarah were greeted most warmly and many words were said, indicating that all were sorry that the two children could not stay longer. Then Anir and Merlin led them out of the Hall, down the corridor, but not to the front door as they were expecting. They went instead to the room of the Stone of Gardar.

"Now you will see and experience something of Merlin's magic," said Anir, "farewell until this time a week hence. Do not fail us and especially not *you*, Peter."

Anir said this with yet another of those funny looks! What could he and Gwyn-ap-Nudd be up to? What was it they wanted from him?

Peter and Sarah watched as Merlin drew a triangle in the air with his staff. He was standing almost directly in front of the Stone. Its green light flickered and grew stronger. Almost instantaneously they felt themselves sucked towards the Stone which appeared to have grown. They were surrounded by bright light for just a few seconds, then felt the wind blow on their faces and a few spots of drizzle. They were outside Arx Emain and back at the bus stop.

CHAPTER FOUR

Plans

The weather had turned cold and wet. Peter and Sarah just stood where they were for two or three minutes before they recovered themselves and their wits.

"Good golly!" said Peter at last, "If that's a demonstration of how the stone works, it's more like something out of a science fiction movie."

"Yeah!" said Sarah, "I think we just got 'beamed'."

They were silent again and stood right where they had been set down, not moving until the bus arrived about ten minutes later.

Getting on to the bus and searching for their tickets jolted Peter into a semblance of normality. As soon as they both sat down and had arranged themselves to continue the journey to Fishguard, Peter looked at his watch.

"It is five minutes past two," he said, "if we are very lucky we shall just about make it."

They were lucky, as it turned out. In their dizzy state neither Peter nor Sarah had bothered to look at the destination posted on the front of the bus. Further enquiries made to the driver established that, not only was the bus going to Fishguard, but it was also going on to Newport. They would be driven right to the drive that led to their cottage. True, they had had to augment their fares, but it was only small change. What mattered was that they would be home for tea.

For most of the journey back, the two children talked little. They were still catching their breath after their journey through the Stone and Peter was pondering on some of the strange things, that had been said to him alone by Gwyn and Anir. Eventually Sarah remarked:

"I don't know how we are going to get back to Arx Emain by next Saturday."

"Silly, we shall just have to ask Aunt Myf again."

"Yes, but suppose she doesn't want to go shopping in Haverfordwest next week? Suppose Catrin is ill? Suppose..."

"Suppose nothing. You just wait and see Sister mine, just wait and see!" Peter sounded hopeful, "anyway, you've changed your tune, haven't you? I thought you did not want to go."

"Well," replied Sarah, rather uncertainly, "if it works as quick as that then maybe we wouldn't have to stay too long. We could just stay long enough to meet Arthur..."

"Then you *do* want to go?"

"Well, just as long as they don't want me to be a spy. OK then, yes, perhaps I do, a little bit."

Sarah gave in gracefully. The two of them then sat back and enjoyed the rest of their journey home.

At three o'clock precisely, Sarah crept into the kitchen and put the kettle on for Father. Dr. Jones was very pleased to have them safely back again, for like Aunt Myf he had the germ of a suspicion at the back of his mind that Peter and Sarah were up to something. However, on this occasion he was just too busy at the University to find out what that something was. After they all telephoned Mother. Grandmother was improving, thank goodness! Mother told them that although she was getting better, Grandmother would have to be in the hospital for another week at least.

"Then I shall have to see that she settles in at home. Everything all right at your end, Darlings?"

They all assured Mother that it was.

"Everything is just fine!" Father told her and as far as he knew, it was.

Sunday passed quietly. Peter, Sarah and Father joined Aunt Myf, Uncle Tomos and Catrin for morning Church and Sunday luncheon afterwards. Then it was Monday and school again. Tuesday and Wednesday were uneventful, except for an unexpected PE lesson on Tuesday afternoon. This was especially designed to annoy Sarah, who hated anything to do with PE.

"Can't understand you," said Peter, over tea at Aunt Myf's. "Most normal people would much rather play hockey in the rain than do a maths test," which had been Peter's fate.

Then on Thursday evening everything changed, for the worse as far as Dr. Jones was concerned and for the better, as far as Peter and Sarah were concerned. The first they knew that something was up, was when Father was very much later than usual coming to fetch them from Aunt Myf's house. Uncle Tomos had been at home for half an hour and Aunt Myf had offered them supper.

"John, whatever is the matter?" enquired Aunt Myf, when Father finally arrived. "You look just about all in! The children were going to join us in a nice lamb hot pot. There is more than enough for you also. That's right! Peter, you set your Father a place and Sarah, you go and get another cup, saucer and plate." Aunt Myf began to ladle out the hot stew.

When everyone was settled, Father thanked Aunt Myf and Uncle Tomos for their hospitality and told them what had detained him.

"Yes, it's been an awful day," he said, "half my department is down with gastric 'flu and we have a weekend of special lectures coming up for people who do most of their degree work at home. Even worse, there are some dignitaries coming to inspect the courses on behalf of their foreign students. We can't let *them* down."

"Will *you* have to be there?" Peter asked.

His heart leaped! Already he could see the hand of fate, or Merlin, or the Bright Beings who live under the Summer Stars, turning this course of events to their advantage.

"Oh dear me," he replied, "I was going to avoid being there as much as possible, of course. Not any longer than Saturday morning I thought. Now my second in command has come down with *the Bug*. I shall have to give all his lectures as well as mine and oversee the others. Not to mention giving the welcoming and finishing addresses."

"Poor Dad," said Sarah, patting him on the shoulder, "how can we help?"

"Oh you can help by being good children," said Aunt Myf immediately. "You don't have to ask, John. Tomos and I will have Peter and Sarah to stay the weekend and you can pick them up again on Monday night."

"I'm really sorry, Myfanwy," said Father.

And that was that! The matter was settled, the die was cast!

As they all left later that evening, Aunt Myf gave Peter and Sarah a big hug. Then she winked at them very purposefully.

"She is suspicious," Sarah said to Peter, as they packed their weekend bags. It was just before bed time.

"No she's not," said Peter, "if she were, she would have said something, you know how she is."

"Maybe, maybe not, but I still think that she is suspicious."

"Don't forget the Ring."

"I won't," said Sarah, going immediately to look for it.

It was where it always was, at the bottom of her jewellery box.

"Anyway," Peter went on, "on the first point, she can't suspect anything because she can't remember any thing about our last little adventure with the Elves. She's got ambrosia, hasn't she."

"Amnesia, loss of memory, you silly boy! And I *still* say that she's suspicious!"

They slept. The next day neither of them could settle very much to anything. This applied especially to schoolwork, as both of their minds were full of Merlin and Elves and King Arthur. Simultaneously, it seemed, and without really discussing the adventure further, they had both decided to go on the journey into Time.

Before the children left their classes for the last break, Peter had an idea. It was going to be indoor play again. Out of the window, Peter could see heavy rain with hailstones bouncing on the tarmac in the playground. He made straight for the school library. They had *Done* Rome and the Romans last year in History lessons.

"Now where is that book?" Peter muttered, "I'm sure Mr. Evans won't mind if I borrow it for the weekend. Ah! There it is. 'Everyday Life in Roman Britain', great! And I'd better take this one too; 'The Romans in Britain.' That should do it."

Although Peter's class had made a study of the Romans in their history lessons, at the time it had all seemed dreadfully dry and dull. Now that he was about to meet some real Romans, albeit at the decline, if not the fall of their Empire, Peter thought that perhaps a little extra study might be helpful.

Peter took the books and spent the rest of break time reading the first book. When the first bell rang for class again, he stuffed both books into his schoolbag.

Soon, but not soon enough for Peter and Sarah, the afternoon's school came to an end. It was still raining when Aunt Myf came to collect them. She arrived in the car with Catrin strapped into her car seat, gurgling and smiling. Peter and Sarah were overwhelmingly cheerful. After the journey home and tea, they both did their homework; finishing it all by suppertime. Aunt Myf showed them to the guest room.

"You'll have to share, unless you want to go in with Catrin, Sarah?"

"No thanks, Aunty. I'll share with Peter. Even if you do snore, brother dear, it's better than being woken up at two in the morning with Catrin's yelling."

The whole family had supper and then telephoned to Mother. Grandmother continued to improve and Mother said that she hoped to be home very soon. Uncle Tomos had a problem Case at the Police Station and was late home. He had supper late and then disappeared into his study. Catrin was put to bed and Peter and Sarah watched some television. They then prepared for bed.

"Want some cocoa?" Aunt Myf offered, as Peter and Sarah emerged damp and pyjama'd from the bathroom.

"Oh yes please!" they cried, and ran swiftly downstairs and into the kitchen.

It was then that Aunt Myf dropped her bombshell, and Peter and Sarah understood the meaning of the winks. She waited until they were seated at the kitchen table, drinking their cocoa. Then she pounced.

"Right, you two," she said firmly, looking first at Peter and then at Sarah, "you are up to something, I know you are, and I am going to find out what it is... and there's no use denying it!" she added sharply, as both children went bright red.

"Come on," she snapped, "who is going to own up first? Lost your tongues have you? Very well I'll begin and you can continue the story if I am right. Are you sitting comfortably?"

Peter and Sarah nodded. They felt very embarrassed and totally surprised.

"You've been to Arx Emain again, haven't you?"

They were horrified, shocked to the core, but the pair of them could not deny it. Aunt Myf was right and obviously much smarter than they had thought.

"But I thought you didn't remember about the Elves and Arx Emain," Peter blurted out.

"Well, I do," replied their astonishing Aunt, "my memory returned very nicely thank you, just after we all moved houses last year. I couldn't forget Anir anyway, could I? He is our cousin!"

"Whaaaat!" exclaimed Peter and Sarah.

"I'm sure I told you before; I used to play round the old stones when I was a girl and Anir used to come there too. He was much older than I of course, and he was already Apprenticed to The Guardian and going through The Tests. Your Mother only saw him a few times. She did not like the Old Places. Too practical by far she was, and anyway, she preferred shopping for clothes more than old stones, so she didn't often come with me. I learnt a great deal about Arx Emain from Anir, a very great deal. I didn't see anything of the Elves though, not until you two came here for the summer last year."

Once more the alarm bell jangled inside Peter's brain. There it was again, Aunt Myf had just mentioned the words: **Apprentice**, **Guardian** and **Tests**, all in the same breath! How did all these people know what he was thinking? Were they in league somehow? He felt slightly light headed and observed that his hands were clammy with perspiration. He hoped that neither Sarah or his Aunt would notice.

"It's true Aunt Myf, we did go to Arx Emain..." Sarah was saying.

"And now we are in a bit of a fix." Peter continued, trying to recover himself from the shock of being forced to think of the unthinkable and impossible again.

He must concentrate on the job in hand.

"We've simply got to get there again tomorrow," he said.

"We promised," Sarah added.

"Oh really!" exclaimed their Aunt. Sarah wondered if she were cross, but she didn't look cross.

"Gwyn and Merlin want us to help King Arthur," Sarah went on.

"Emperor Arthur, don't forget, he's a Roman Briton," corrected Peter.

"King Arthur? Emperor Arthur? If I didn't know you better, I would think that you were making all this up."

"Gwyn and Merlin are going to use the Miraculous Stone to send us back to the time of the King-Emperor Arthur, so that we can take him the Ring of Invisibility," Peter explained, "then he can conquer all his enemies and we can come home."

"And is it reliable, this Miraculous Stone?"

"Well, Merlin used it to get us back to the bus stop," said Peter, blushing again because, said like that, it sounded rather silly.

"OK then, and?" Aunt Myf did not look entirely convinced.

"Yes, and Mum and Dad came through it after the battle with Arddu," Sarah added eagerly.

"Hmmm!"

"We've GOT to go tomorrow, even if we just give the Ring to Merlin, we've just got to!" they pleaded.

"Do you really *have* to see King Arthur?" Aunt Myf asked, after thinking for a few minutes.

"We don't exactly have to," said Sarah.

"But it would be great!" Peter said, his eyes shining, "just think of it, King Arthur!"

Then Aunt Myf smiled sympathetically. She was weakening.

"I'm almost tempted to come with you myself, I must say!" she said, "if it wasn't for Catrin..."

As if on cue, Catrin woke up and began to yell. Aunt Myf dashed from the kitchen, having whisked a bottle of baby juice out of the fridge and plunged it into hot water. She then took the jug and bottle upstairs. They soon heard the crying cease. Sarah looked at Peter.

"What do you think? Will she let us go?"

"I bet she does, I'm sure she will."

"How on earth did she cotton on?"

"I think she has some kind of sixth sense about it all," said Peter, putting his head in his hands and sighing loudly, "but we have to get the Ring to Merlin. That's the least we can do."

The two of them drank their cocoa and stared at the table. Then they stared at each other, then at the table again. Aunt Myf reappeared in the doorway.

"I will take you to Gwyn-ap-Nudd," she smiled, "of course I will, but I need convincing that the Stone will bring you back, as well as *take* you to another time."

"Oh thank you, thank you!" cried Sarah and Peter.

"Does that mean that you are coming with us to Arx Emain?" said Peter, frowning crossly.

"Don't worry, I'm not about to spoil your fun," laughed Aunt Myf, "I just want to make sure of the lie of the land. Now finish that cocoa and off to bed. I think you will need all the rest you can get."

At that moment, Uncle Tomos came into the kitchen.

"What is all this commotion? Why aren't these young people in bed, Myfanwy?"

"Oh, they are just a little bit excited, Tomos. You see, a friend of mine, who has to do with something concerning the Celtic and Early British History Society, (she meant Gwyn-ap-Nudd!) wants me to make an urgent visit and I have promised that Peter and Sarah may come with me. I am sure it will turn out to be something most worth while. You don't mind having Catrin again, do you my dear?"

"Not at all, but Myfanwy, I thought that you gave up all that Celtic Society stuff when we were married?"

And Uncle Tomos gave her a very *Old Fashioned Look*.

"Oh, this is something quite out of the ordinary, I promise you dear. I expect it will be a *One Off*, so we must go, mustn't we. We will have an early lunch and go afterwards."

She patted her husband on the shoulder. Then she turned to the children.

"Goodnight Peter, goodnight Sarah!"

They knew that they were being sent to bed. Glad to escape any more probing questions, they fled up the stairs. They could just hear Aunt Myf inviting Uncle Tomos to have a cup of cocoa, "To soothe your nerves dear. Now do tell me all about those nasty burglaries..."

Their escape made good, Peter and Sarah fell into bed and slept.

The next day had an almost dream-like quality about it. Peter and Sarah packed up their rucksacks very carefully. Peter's included the books on ancient Rome, a change of clothes some chocolate, a note pad and pen and the teddy that must *never* be mentioned.

Sarah's contained some rather more practical items: a Latin dictionary, a change of clothes, a torch, a pair of old binoculars, a packet of glucose sweets and the Ring of Concealment. Uncle Tomos waved them off after lunch. Peter and Sarah felt very nervous.

"Bye, bye, don't be too long," he called.

"We won't," they replied.

"Well, we might be," Sarah said to her Aunt.

"You had better not be!" Aunt Myf replied, "make no mistake, I shall be monitoring everything. We shall synchronise watches and ready or not, I will tell Gwyn to bring you back. Also, I shall only let you go on one condition."

"What's that?" Sarah and Peter groaned.

"You are only going if Anir goes with you."

"Ah!," Peter sighed with relief, "I thought you were going to suggest something really awful."

"I might, if you mess about," said Aunt Myf, with surprising gravity. "With Catrin so little, I do not have time for messing about especially on the whims of Elves and children."

"Don't be cross Aunty," Sarah pleaded.

"Well, you could just give Merlin that Ring."

"Yes, I know but..." began Peter.

"Yes, and I know too! Come on you two, by the looks of things we have arrived. I think that must be your friend Merlin over there."

Merlin stood to one side of the bus stop, exactly where Peter and Sarah had been left the week before. Aunt Myf managed to park off the road and they all got out. Peter and Sarah gathered together jackets and rucksacks while Aunt Myf locked the car up.

"I do hope it will be safe," she said, then, "good afternoon, sir," she said to Merlin.

Merlin bowed low before her.

"I did not know that you would be bringing an older sister," he said, bowing also to Sarah and Peter.

Sarah giggled. Aunt Myf went quite pink.

"This is our Aunt Myfanwy," Peter said, by way of introduction.

Merlin then said to them, smiling brightly:

"I am so glad that you have arrived on time. Please follow me."

He turned away and walked off into the rough scrub land. After a few yards, he stopped, described a triangle in the air with his staff, muttered some strange words and...

"I'm flying," Aunt Myf thought.

"Wow, it's the Stone again," thought Peter and Sarah.

Suddenly, there they all were in the Golden Room that housed the Miraculous Stone of the Elves. The Stone glowed bright green within its niche and sitting on the ornate golden throne that stood before it was Gwyn-ap-Nudd.

"All present?" he enquired, "then welcome, Merlin and friends! Welcome Sarah and Peter! I see that you have Myfanwy with you also. We are honoured, most honoured."

"Thank you, My Lord Gwyn," replied Aunt Myf, curtseying, "I have come to see that my sister's children are properly looked after and that after any adventures undertaken, they are returned safely to their own time."

"But Lady," Merlin interrupted, "you have just experienced the Magic of the stone yourself, and survived."

"Yes," cried Peter, "and look, look at the time on your watch Aunty."

Peter had observed before, that the journey to Arx Emain from
the bus stop appeared to take no time at all. Being of an
enquiring mind, as soon as Merlin got out his staff, Peter had
timed the whole event. It took no time at all. The hands on his
watch stayed still.

"All right everybody, I declare that I'm impressed. BUT, I have
one more condition before I consent to let you go on this madcap
adventure."

"And I want to know what Merlin has brought us from King
Arthur," cried Sarah.

"First things first, little Lady," Gwyn smiled, "let your Aunt tell
me of this condition, although I know it already."

Aunt Myf blushed.

"I want Anir to go as their protector," she said.

"Do you not trust Merlin?" Gwyn waved an arm towards the
wizard.

"It isn't that I don't trust him, really it isn't," replied Aunt Myf.
"It's just that I would feel easier in my mind if I knew that Anir
was with them. Seeing as how he's family in a way, however
distant."

"Very well," said Gwyn. "Anir shall be summoned."

The Elf Lord shut his eyes for a moment, then said:

"It is done. He will be with us soon. I am sure he will be more
than willing to guard you once again. Now then Merlin, you may
show Peter and Sarah what you have brought here that belongs
to King Arthur."

The children watched, fascinated, as Merlin felt in various
pockets. Finally he produced a small silver ornament. It was
shaped like an egg, with a flat bottom on it. At the top a helmeted
face showed. The figure was dressed like a Roman legionary.

"Why, it's a little man," said Sarah, as Merlin passed it to her.

"I know what it is," Peter said, when his turn came to inspect
it, "it's a chess piece, isn't it Merlin. It's one of the knights."

77

"You are quite correct," Merlin replied, "but let me have it back please. It comes from a very special chess set of which the King is extremely fond. If he knew that I had taken one of the pieces, there's no knowing what he would do to me!"

"It certainly looks very fine," said Aunt Myf peering at it, "so you had better take it back at once if it is *that* valuable, and these two madcaps with you."

She looked round, to see Aneryn with Anir standing in the doorway. Anir looked ready for action. He was booted and cloaked, with his long, two handed sword at his side.

"Before you ask, Peter and Sarah, I am very glad to be your companion on this very special journey."

"Anir!" they both cried, and ran towards him.

"Good!" said Merlin, "are we all ready then?"

"Just hold on a second," said Aunt Myf. "I checked this watch with the news on the wireless this morning. I make it twelve thirty exactly. I want you both back here by five thirty exactly. Six o'clock at the very latest, or Uncle Tomos will be ringing his friends at the police station. It would be very embarrassing for me to have the police searching for us all, just because you were late! It would also mean big trouble for you, so keep an eye on your watches! At six o'clock, if you are not here by then, I shall ask Gwyn to bring you back, and I don't care what you are doing or what is going on, understand?"

"Yes Aunt Myf," Peter and Sarah replied sheepishly.

Then Sarah ran to her and gave her a kiss, Peter gave her a hug and they picked up their rucksacks.

"We're ready now," they said.

"You stand by me, Myfanwy," said the Lord Gwyn-ap-Nudd. "Anir, Peter, Sarah, you must go and stand by Merlin, near to the Stone of Gardar."

As before, Merlin made a triangle in the air with his wizard's staff. The glowing light surrounding the miraculous object grew stronger.

"Farewell!" called Gwyn and Aunt Myf.

The stone grew large and the portal in its upper third began to widen.

"Good bye-eeeeeeeeeeee!" Sarah and Peter replied, as they were drawn through the Miraculous Stone of Gardar and into the tunnel of bright lights that leads to The Land of Summer Stars.

CHAPTER FIVE

At The Camp In Gaul

It was dark. In fact, it was very dark. For a moment, Sarah wondered if the Miraculous Stone of Gardar had not made a mistake and put them out somewhere in outer space. Peter wondered if he had been suddenly struck blind. It was rather annoying.

"All here?" it was Merlin's voice.

"Yes," all replied.

"Splendid! Now then, I am afraid there is no moon tonight, and it is rather cloudy anyway. Put your hands out. You can hold on to my cloak if you can't see; Peter, Sarah. It is nothing to worry about, your eyes will get used to the dark eventually. Come on! The Stone has put us down near to where I left for Britain yesterday. It is not far to Arthur's camp."

They went a few paces forward, very slowly. The ground seemed to be rough and the children stumbled in the dark. The only person who did not stumble was Anir, who was used to finding his way at night.

"Merlin?"

"Yes Peter."

"Where are we exactly?"

"Exactly, Hmmm, let me see, exactly... Exactly, we are about half a mile outside Autun, which is where the Emperor Arthur has his fortified camp at present."

"And where is that?" Sarah asked.

"Somewhere in the middle to bottom end of Gaul," the wizard replied with a sigh, "questions, questions, all these questions. You must wear your teachers out!"

"But where's Gaul?" Sarah asked again.

"Don't you know THAT," interrupted Peter, "it is what they used to call France of course, you silly!"

"FRANCE! What on earth are we doing in France?" wailed Sarah, completely confused.

"We are here because this is where the enemy is," answered Merlin, suddenly bringing their discussion to an end. "Please look out, everyone. The ground slopes away quite steeply just here, do be careful."

"If only it wasn't so dark," said Peter.

"Hang on, it needn't be," cried Sarah. "Stop everybody, I have just the very thing!"

They all stopped walking and stood by curiously, while Sarah took off her rucksack and felt around in it for her torch. At last it was found.

"It would have to be right down at the bottom," she muttered. She brought it out, found Merlin's hand and gave him the torch.

"What is this?" he asked.

"It's a torch, I mean, it is a machine that makes light."

"You modern people seem to have machines to do everything," Merlin said, with a slightly scornful tone in his voice. "You will have to show me how to use it. I am not familiar with this light machine."

He shook it hard.

"Oh, don't do that. The batteries will fall out. Look, there's a little switch, just here."

Sarah put Merlin's finger on it and pushed it on... and off... and on again.

"My thanks to you, Sarah, we may go along now a little quicker."

Merlin plunged down the wooded hillside at a greatly increased pace, so much so, that Peter and Sarah had great difficulty in following him.

"I'm sure we won't be quick enough for Aunt Myf," thought Peter, "we only have five hours. We shall just get to see King Arthur and say 'hello' and then it will be time to go home. What a nuisance."

Aloud he said:

"I wonder what the time is?"

He could not make it out on his watch.

Anir had travelled so far in complete silence. He was engrossed in listening and observing and thinking. He now answered Peter.

82

"The time? It is about one hour before dawn. My guess is that we will pass into Arthur's Camp quite a bit before true sunrise."

"You are most observant, friend Anir. I want Arthur to meet you before anyone else does."

"Why?" asked Sarah.

"Because, just at the moment, you both look a little too strange for your own good. You will need a disguise to start with."

"Oh!"

"Then you will need to familiarise yourself with life in the camp, our ways and customs, so that you may blend into the background. Arthur and I agreed on an alias if you did happen to accompany the Ring of Concealment. Our story is that you are children of some distant relation of Arthur's. The Roman Emperor Odovacer has taken your parents prisoner. This means that everyone in the Camp will be very sympathetic to you while with us. It also explains why you are travelling with us for the present. There! What do you think?"

"It's very clever," said Sarah, "but when does The Ring come into it?"

"Ho, ho! Steady on little maid," laughed Merlin, "first things first! You have a great deal to get used to before then. Remember you are now 1,500 years before *your* time. Most of life, here and now, is very different from that to which you are accustomed. Although, even so, you will find that the people are much the same."

They all walked on in silence for quite a while. Somehow Sarah could not get her brain round the fact that she was in France, and ancient France, or Gaul at that! Peter was thinking about Time...

They had so much to do and so little time in which to do it. Only five hours, and it must be even less by now. How did time work here? Did it slow down or stop as it appeared to do when they travelled via the Stone, or didn't it? How long had they been walking?

Peter held his wristwatch up to his ear. It was a really good watch, one of those that you could go diving in, if you wanted to. It had just had a new battery put in it last week, so Peter expected it to last at least another year before stopping. Yes, he could hear it go 'tick, tick.' All was well. When it was light enough, the first thing he was going to do was to check the time on his watch.

At last, a pale glow showed over the hills to the east. A breeze sighed in the trees around them.

"Dawn is coming," said Anir.

"Nearly there," Merlin said encouragingly, "if you look down there and to the left, you may begin to see the town of Autun." Peter and Sarah looked. I am afraid to say that they were not much impressed.

"It's not as big as Haverfordwest," whispered Sarah.

"It's not as big as Newport, and the buildings seem to look rather the worse for wear. Those larger buildings over there are all in bits."

What was left of the civic buildings in Autun were hardly impressive, although they must have been so once. The temples to the gods, the basilicas, the baths, the walls and fortifications, the great arena and latterly, the churches, had all come in for a pasting by parties of marauding barbarians.

"And so would you be too in bits, if the Goths had been attacking you for the past several years!" Merlin told them with much feeling, "but here is *our* camp, The Emperor Arthur's Camp!" Merlin said proudly, continuing his guided tour, "look; down by the river there."

This time they were rather more impressed. The camp was absolutely huge. It looked like a spread out fort or castle. Built in squares and rectangles and holding a great many tents and wooden huts, it was practically as big as the town beyond.

"Gosh! Arthur must have an enormous army," said Sarah.

"Oh, only several thousands, about twenty or thirty thousand," said Merlin, airily, "not all Britons or from Britain, of course; a great many are our allies. Lucius, our enemy, has more. I heard someone say the other day, that he has twelve legions, with nearly seven thousand men in each legion. I do hope that is an exaggeration, but our scouts will soon find out if it is true!"

They were passing swiftly down the hill, towards the river. Only a little further and they would arrive at the partly fortified gates of Arthur's Camp. It was growing lighter by the minute. Merlin returned Sarah's torch. Peter tried looking at his watch but could not quite make out the hands. They walked on in complete silence, not wishing to attract undue attention from even the friendliest of eyes.

The fortified Camp gates loomed large out of the morning mists that rise by great rivers at dawn. There were guards on the gate. From what he could remember from school history lessons, Peter thought they looked like the pictures of legionaries, only their shields were flatter and rounder. They saluted Merlin. One of them spoke in a language that was quite unintelligible to Peter or Sarah. Was it Greek, British, Celt or Latin? Their spirits sank as they began to realise that possibly no-one spoke English here, but then Merlin pointed his staff at them and they found that they were able to understand everything.

"Cool," thought Sarah, "that staff, or wand, or whatever it is, would come in jolly handy at school. I would soon be top in French. I do wish I had one of those!"

"I was just introducing you to Marcus here," said Merlin, pointing his staff at the guard. "I am telling him about all the rotten things the soldiers of Lucius Iberius have done to your family."

Peter and Sarah nodded, as if seeming to agree.

"You had better take them straight to Arthur," said Marcus. "Poor things! The Emperor will be awake now as it is almost sunrise."

And indeed, the first rays began to appear above the glowing ball, which showed itself from behind a distant hill. Peter, Sarah and Anir followed Merlin up the track to the Camp gate and through it to the Camp beyond. What a marvel it was! The serried ranks of tents, made of some kind of animal hide or skins, were arranged most precisely in regular patterns, as was ever the Roman way. They were quite large tents, and as Merlin told them, there were at least eight men inside each one. Peter and Sarah could hardly take it all in. They marched up what seemed to be a main road leading to a wide space.

"This is the Forum or parade ground," Merlin said in explanation.

"I thought that the Forum was in Rome," Sarah whispered.

"No," said Peter, "most Roman towns had one, and I gather that Roman camps had them too."

"But Arthur is BRITISH!"

"Sarah, weren't you paying ANY attention to what Merlin was saying at Arx Emain?"

"Yes, really I was, but being put down in Ancient France has got me seriously confused. Where is Camelot? That's what I want to know."

"If there is one, it will be back in Britain, I mean Britannia. But I have a funny feeling that there wasn't one; isn't one, I mean. Oh dear, now I'm getting confused!"

"Ssh!"

Anir prodded them forward towards the most enormous, most grand, most richly decorated tent in the whole camp.

"This is the Praetorium!" Merlin proudly announced, "or if you like, the Headquarters of the whole Army; the Generals', Officers' and our Emperor's temporary home!"

86

They were all standing before the entrance to the tent. Merlin took his staff and knocked with it on one of the tent posts.

"Come in," said a voice, "I know it's you, Merlin," and they all went inside.

There before them was the young Arthur. He was a young man of about twenty years or so. He was very tall. Quite a bit taller than Anir whom Peter and Sarah thought to be well over six feet. He had short, curly black hair, was clean shaven and had steely blue eyes.

"Wow!" thought Sarah, "he's really handsome. Much better looking than any of the film actors who have played him."

"What a leader!" Peter was thinking. "He looks to be awfully strong, terribly fit and I don't think he needs weight lifting lessons at any gym."

King, or was it Emperor Arthur had turned round to face them. He had a rough towel in his hand. A bowl of steaming water stood on a table. They had caught him at his toilet; washing to get ready for the day and its duties. Like all the good Romans before him, he took great care over his appearance.

"Good morning Merlin and friends. And whom do we have here?"

"I have brought Peter and Sarah."

Peter bowed and Sarah curtseyed.

"And this is Anir, The Guardian of all the lands in the Domain belonging to the Kingdom of Gwyn-ap-Nudd, Lord of the Elves."

Anir bowed low. Introductions over, Arthur finished drying himself off and went to find the leather corselet that went over his tunic.

"Gwyn-ap-Nudd. Ah yes, I must look him up when we get back home. He could prove a useful ally. Merlin, you will remind me to do that."

"I shall not forget, Highness."

The young Emperor continued to get himself ready.

"Where on earth is my other boot? I'm sorry Peter, Sarah and Anir, I have an awful lot to get through today and any minute now *they* will all be in here, wanting to know what to do next! Now, if you will... Ah there it is! Under my bed all the time."

He retrieved the boot and put it on. They were beautiful red leather boots and he was obviously rather proud of them.

"As I was just going to say, Peter and Sarah, you are to be my long lost cousins. We nobles always have hoards of 'em. Makes inheritance that much more interesting. You Anir had better be a long lost Uncle, or something. You are staying with me while we search for your parents who have been captured by Lucius Iberius. We could say that they are up for ransom. Enemies are always doing that these days. It makes money for their next campaign."

"That is our cover story, all right," said Peter, "but don't we look a bit odd?"

"Of course you do. How stupid of me! Merlin, do you see that chest by my bed? Just pull it out will you. That's it! Peter and Sarah; if you look inside, you will find appropriate clothes for your disguise."

They went over to the chest and pulled several tunics and cloaks. There were also several pairs of sandals to try. When they were both accoutred Roman style, Arthur walked around them.

"A definite improvement, I think. Strange clothes you wear in the future! By the way, Merlin, I wanted to ask you; am I allowed to visit the future?"

"I am not sure at present. We will think about it when you have won your next battle."

"Then I AM going to win!"

Arthur gave a broad grin. He was pleased at having wrung a prediction out of Merlin who was noted for being tight with information.

"I didn't say that," Merlin said crossly.

"I'm going to win! I'm going to win! Oh Merlin, you are so exasperating sometimes. Sarah, have you brought the Ring of Concealment?"

He turned and looked at Sarah with his piercing blue eyes. She dug down into the bottom of her rucksack.

"Here it is," she said, passing it over to Arthur.

Arthur put it on.

"How does it work?" he said. Sarah showed him.

"You have to turn it round and close your fist over the jewel."

"Like this?" Arthur disappeared.

"Yes, just like that."

"Oh this is fun! Look Merlin, I can tickle you from behind and you can't see me!" Merlin gave a jump.

"Arthur!" he said, sounding annoyed.

The young Emperor reappeared and gave the Ring back to Sarah.

"That is likely to be a formidable weapon. Hide it for us, Sarah, until the time comes when our plans are ripe. You had better, both of you, put these funny clothes of yours inside your funny bags. Use these instead."

Arthur passed the children a large bag made of leather each. "You can put your supplies and treasures in these. I will keep all your things in my special chest. No one DARES to touch anything in there, do they, Merlin?"

"Oh no, certainly not. They would not dream of it," Merlin replied, frowning and looking very guilty.

The children wondered if Arthur knew about the borrowed chess piece. Merlin then continued, brazenly:

"However, speaking of treasures, one of your chess pieces seems to have fallen out of its box. Here..."

He passed the silver knight to Arthur. Arthur gave Merlin a knowing look, but he just said:

"Thank you Merlin," and replaced the chess piece in its box inside the chest.

"And now for breakfast. I am feeling particularly hungry and I expect you are too."

He clapped his hands and in came a golden haired youth, bearing a large dish with bread cakes, cheese and apples on it. "Thank you, Osric, and we shall have some hot spiced wine as well as water today, and more bread please."

Osric bowed to his Lord and left hurriedly, reappearing soon after with the drinks and more food.

"I suppose this makes a change from tea and toast," said Sarah.

"Or coffee and Cornflakes," laughed Peter.

He looked at his watch. Amazingly, only two and a half minutes had elapsed.

"Thank goodness!" he thought, "if time goes as slowly as this, we might be able to spend several days here."

Outside the tent the Camp began to stir. Horses neighed in the cavalry lines and there were sounds from the other animals that were in Arthur's camp: cows, sheep, pigs and chickens, so that it sounded like a noisy farm. The soldiers began to go about their duties. Servants and others began the task of feeding vast numbers and armourers could be heard attending to the dents and knocks sustained in previous battles. When Arthur had finished his own breakfast he smiled cheerfully at his guests. "And now to the business of the day," he said.

Now, his manner had been so easy and pleasant, positively laid back, as Sarah thought; that the two children had almost forgotten that they were on a mission.

"I beg your leave, fair cousins; I shall call you cousins for the duration of this venture. I regret that I must presently hold a meeting with my generals, officers and the leaders of our allied troops. Thus, Merlin, I call upon you to take our guests around the Camp, so that they may see and know and perhaps marvel at our might. At the end of one hour please bring them back to us. There will be arrangements to be made, and I have the feeling that things will move swiftly from now on. Farewell to you all until then."

Merlin opened the tent flap and shooed them out. It was a lovely hot summer's day.

"Better and better!" cried Peter. "We left home in winter and here we are in summer!"

"You should have brought sunblock with you, brother dear," Sarah remarked, "it looks like today is going to be a scorcher."

"If it is, I would not like to be any of them," said Anir, as he pointed out some rather young looking soldiers being drilled by their sergeants.

Many were wearing armour that was made of metal layers, some wore chain mail, some wore leather jerkins and it all looked extremely hot and heavy. They carried round flat shields and short swords. The gladius was still the chief infantry weapon of any half decent Roman army and a very effective one too!

"We will walk around the Intervallum," said Merlin, "then you will see the whole of the Camp at a glance, so to speak."

"What is the *Intervallum*?" asked Sarah.

"It is a space between two things. In this case, a space between the ramparts and the tents of the Camp itself," Merlin replied. "As you may observe by the state of the ramparts, our fortifications have been made in rather too much of a hurry. They need to be improved, especially if it turns out that Arthur has to fight the Roman Emperor as well as his Consul. We have to be strong enough here to withstand a long siege, if necessary."

He turned down what looked like the main road round the Camp. On either side the cavalrymen were seeing to their horses. Then the Wizard turned left and into the wide gap between the fence and the tents.

"Intervallum, Intervallum!" muttered Sarah. "If it's the interval, Peter, when do we get the chocolates and ice creams?"

"Silly goose!" was all the reply Sarah had from her brother, "I brought a note book, Sis, and when we get back I'm going to make a plan of this Camp. It will be *Brill* at school I bet."

Thus, Merlin took Peter, Sarah and Anir around the Camp. There had been plenty of horses and plenty of armour to look at, but none looked anything like what Sarah had imagined. Some of the older soldiers greeted them. One or two of the legionaries complained to them. Although the army was a good life, they said, it was not like the Good Old Days.

"When Britain was the home of some of the greatest Legions the Empire ever had!" one said. "Ah! We were tough then, all right! We used to march thirty miles a day with a full pack on our backs to fight a battle and if you didn't go quick enough, they flogged you. March or die, that's what!"

"You're right you are," said another, "discipline was much better then. We'd march and march, and then we'd have to make camp from scratch every night. And drill? We'd drill for hours and hours and then we'd have to dig ditches and ramparts, or even build bridges! And those Centurions? Well they could really give orders! Their shouting could be heard from here to Rome, I tell you! These young ones don't know they're born!"

"But The Lord Arthur is a good leader."

"Aye, one of the best. He's one that cares about his men, he does."

And so the conversation went on, the Old Legionaries agreeing most pleasantly with each other.

Merlin's party moved on.

"So many tents," Peter whispered to Anir, "and so many different groups."

"Yes," answered Anir, "I guess that the main troops of Arthur's army are Roman Britons as he is, from either our own Islands or from the mainland. Little Britannia across the sea, I believe they call it, or Armorica."

"Well, I think it's all completely and utterly mystifying!" interrupted Sarah.

"Then," continued Anir, ignoring her, "there will be Arthur's allies. People he has called upon to help him fight the Proconsul Lucius. They might come from anywhere in the Roman Empire and probably do."

"How do you know that?" Sarah asked him.

"Because Gwyn-ap-Nudd has told me about that time," explained Anir simply, "remember, he lived through that age. It is only one out of many that he has experienced. It holds no surprises for him, only for us who do not know it."

"Do you know what is going to happen then?" asked Peter.

"Perhaps... perhaps not," Anir replied enigmatically.

"You are very mysterious, Anir," Sarah said, "don't you find this all very mysterious Peter?"

"But it's exciting, Sis! I wouldn't miss this for anything. It's all so different."

They passed the cavalry lines again, where the horses were being tended to by their riders. Although, if the horses belonged to officers, they were fed and watered by servants. Peter and Sarah saw that the cavalry soldiers were dressed and equipped differently to the foot soldiers; having lighter armour, a smaller shield, a longer sword and a lance. There were many more riders now in Arthur's legion than formerly. The art of war was beginning to change and the young leader tried hard to keep up with the times.

The Generals of the Emperor Arthur and their troops endeavoured to maintain the customs of the old Roman army as much as possible. However, they too were not dressed as heavily or uniformly as the soldiers had been under the old Emperors: Augustus, Trajan, or even Constantine. Eventually, then, Peter and Sarah found themselves once more walking down the Via Praetoria, or the main road that led to Arthur's Headquarters.

When they came near Arthur's tent they could hear men's voices raised in animated discussion. Merlin tapped on the tent pole, but this time he did not wait outside but went straight inside. Besides Arthur, there were several other men in the tent who were obviously his Generals; chieftains of some kind or another. They were seated on benches at a table. There were also some other soldiers (Centurions perhaps?) in armour standing round.

"Waiting for their daily orders," thought Peter.

He suddenly felt immensely excited and wished he were old enough to be among them.

"Gormant, my half brother; Flergant, King of Armorica; Kaw, Lord of the North Britons; Henwyneb, my old friend; Gyssevin, my champion; Kai and Bedwyr, please greet my cousins and Anir, their uncle," said Arthur.

The chieftains nodded and smiled at them. The two *cousins* bowed to the assembly and waited to see what would happen next. Unperturbed, Merlin went straight to the table upon which lay a parchment map.

"Well then, Arthur, what are you going to do?"

"Gormant says that the prisoners of the first skirmish are safely on their way to Paris. However, he has brought some others back here."

"What a nuisance! Extra mouths to feed. Still, they may have their uses."

"One of them has been very useful already. Gormant tells me that one of them says: not only that there are less of them than we had first thought, but that Lucius Iberius is on his way to Langres right now."

"Splendid!" said Merlin.

"Oh, is it, why?"

94

"Well of course it is, my dear Arthur. If he marches into Langres then he is probably going to come back here. But you could find that out for certain and then lay your plans."

Merlin peered at the map.

"It would be excellent if you were able to cut him off here."

The wizard made a stabbing motion at some spot on the map that Sarah and Peter could not see.

"But first," he continued, "you will probably have to send a scouting party to Langres with a fair number of spies attached. Yes, it seems vital that you find out where Lucius will go next. Then you may be able to trap the insolent tax collector!"

"Would-be insolent tax collector," corrected Arthur. "All those in favour of sending a spying party to Langres raise your hands."

All did so.

"Fine, no abstentions then. That would seem to be fairly conclusive. The only thing we have left to decide is: who will go to Langres? Will you Gormant?"

A huge man got up from the table. Peter presumed that it must be Gormant.

"I will go," he said, "the best in my Legion will go with me, but as to the spies... they must be volunteers."

Anir stepped forward at once:

"I am used to passing through this place and that unnoticed," he said.

"That is one spy for our mission, thank you, Anir," said Arthur.

"I would like to go too," Peter said excitedly, determined now upon seeing some action.

"No!" returned Merlin sharply and suddenly, "I have been thinking this over. I say no! You must be our guests, Peter and Sarah, not combatants and certainly not spies. Our enemies are not over kind to spies, if and when they find them."

"Then I will find someone from my troops," said Flergant.

"And I will make up the remainder from my army," added Kaw.

"Very good," said Arthur, "then make all ready!"

He was well pleased at the result of this meeting. The Generals and other officers got up to leave and the gathering broke up. After they had all gone, Arthur turned to Anir.

"You are not bound to go," he said.

"I will go all the same," Anir replied.

"Then Sarah had better give her Ring to you," said Peter.

"Very well, will you give it back to me?" asked Anir, looking hard at her.

Most willingly she passed the Ring of Concealment over to him.

"Merlin, see that Anir and the others have all they need for the journey," said the Emperor Arthur.

"Aye, Lord," said Merlin, and led Anir, Sarah and Peter out of the tent.

"You two wait here," the wizard told them sternly.

"Bother!" said Peter, under his breath, "I really *did* want to go too."

"I shall return 'ere long to bid you farewell," said Anir.

Then, as soon as Merlin turned his back, he winked at the two children and suddenly passed the Ring back to Peter.

"Back soon!" he hissed at them and walked off behind Merlin.

"That's a turn up for the books, and no mistake!" breathed Peter, very much surprised.

"Does he mean you to go too?"

"I don't know, Sarah, but it looks hopeful. He must have overheard my whisper."

"He must have done. But I don't know if... now that it comes to it, I can let you go."

"Don't worry Sis, I've got the Ring. It'll all be fine, you'll see!"

And so saying, Peter and Sarah sat down in front of King Arthur's tent to wait and see what might happen next.

CHAPTER SIX

Spies For Arthur

As they sat outside Arthur's tent, Peter and Sarah could hear Arthur talking to Osric. It was nothing exciting. He just ordered lunch, or Prandium, as they called it in Roman times, for himself and his guests. Peter and Sarah gathered that luncheon was going to be similar to breakfast, with the addition of hard boiled eggs, fish and vegetables.

"This is boring," Sarah remarked flatly. "I thought it was going to be much more exciting than this."

"Hang on, Sarah. We've only been here a couple of hours."

Peter looked at his watch. It said twelve thirty six, the time at home in modern Britain. The two watched Arthur's soldiers getting on with their work. Presently, some of them marched on to the forum and began to drill again, almost exactly as Peter had seen people do on the television films about army life at home. It did look very boring. The Centurions shouted loudly and often at their men as they marched them up and down. Peter was glad that he was not one of them.

Osric came out of the tent and disappeared off towards the back of the Camp. Everybody seemed to have something to do, except for Peter and Sarah. Even Anir had been taken off to prepare for the journey to Langres.

Various people visited Arthur during the next hour, including Gormant, who came to give a full report on the previous day's battles and to plan the spying mission in greater detail. This was interesting, to Peter at least! He sat himself closer to the tent in order to listen. Engrossed in the conversation of others, Peter did not notice Sarah get up and walk off.

"I'm fed up," she had thought, "I think I shall go and see if I can find Anir. Peter won't mind."

So she got up quietly from her place by the tent and wandered about the Camp like a tourist. At the back of the tents she found the ovens, where bread and pastries were being baked by the servants and camp women, and on which the midday meal was cooking. Although, they were hardly ovens as Sarah knew them; they were more like stone-ringed camp fires with the kitchen pots and pans put on the top of them.

Then she went to inspect the Bath House and Latrines! These also turned out to be not at all what Sarah expected. The Bath House was very similar to those she had once visited in Bath, only much smaller and plainer. The Latrines, which she described to Peter later as a matter of some urgency, were almost unbearable, unless perhaps you were a soldier and used to the indelicate! She passed quickly by these last, and then found a man with a big anvil who was trying to ease a dent in someone's helmet.

Sarah stood and watched the smith work for some time. She thought the whole process interesting and liked watching the sparks fly into the air when the hammer came down upon the metal. Then she went to look at the tents of Arthur's allies, where some very strange looking people were stationed. Arthur must have had an extremely wide circle of friends ready and willing to help him. Unfortunately, Anir was nowhere to be seen.

"I can't imagine where he can be," Sarah thought, somewhat crossly.

At last, she decided to return to the tent, only to find that Peter had gone.

"Where is that brother of mine?" she began to mutter under her breath.

Sarah walked all round the tent in her frustration. Then, round the final corner she almost ran straight into Peter and Anir. Peter was smiling and looking extremely excited.

"Anir says that I can go after all. Isn't it great!"

"But only if you do exactly what I say," warned Anir. "I can't take bits and pieces of you back to Aunt Myf."

"I solemnly promise to do whatever you tell me to do," Peter said, holding up his right hand, "just as long as I can go with you, *please?*"

"In that case, you had better make sure that you are completely ready by after lunch. I have taken enough food for two in my saddlebags, so that is taken care of. We shall only be away overnight, assuming that all goes to plan. I do need some extra bread though, Sarah, be a good girl and go to where the ovens are. They are still making bread for the soldiers' midday meal. Go and ask one of the bakers for a couple of extra rolls each."

"OK," said Sarah, and sped away.

"Now Peter, I want to make sure that you understand what you are about to undertake. Someone small, who can go silently has to go very close to, if not right inside, the headquarters of Lucius Iberius. That is of course, assuming we can actually get safely inside the town of Langres."

Peter's stomach sank. He suddenly had a niggling feeling that Anir wanted him to be that someone. Was this why he had sent Sarah to the other end of the Camp? If she found out that this was the plan, Peter was sure that Sarah would 'freak out' and refuse to let him go at all. Perhaps Anir knew that.

Then, within a deep cranny of his brain, there was another question to be answered. Did Peter really trust Anir to keep him safe during such a trial? When Anir spoke again, he answered this last query in part.

"Perhaps it is better if Sarah does not know the full details of our secret mission until our return. You and I should be quite safe with the Ring of Concealment. At any rate, if you do not want to trust yourself to me and my Ring that is fair enough. You are quite free to take up this offer of adventure, or not. If not, then I shall just have to do the job by myself, although I think it might prove good enough as a **Test** for you."

Peter momentarily ignored Anir's last remark about a Test. He had enough to think about with thoughts of becoming a spy, however temporary that might prove to be! With all the excitement going on around him, it was easy to forget about the adventure being a *Test* until much later.

"Let me think it over, Anir."

"Very well."

"I've thought! I'll do it. I *do* trust you enough Anir to know that you will keep me safe and bring me back. But what will Sarah do while we are away?"

"I am sure that Merlin will look after her, and Arthur too. However, what does she think of you leaving her here alone? We should ask her when she arrives with the bread."

The two conspirators did not have to wait long. Two minutes later, Sarah returned with the rolls and Anir stowed them away in his bag. Then Anir and Peter told her most of what they had been discussing. For a little while she pretended to be angry at them for leaving her alone, but then she admitted that she was too nervous to go on such a trip.

"I don't think I would even like to go as far as the outskirts of Langres, never mind into the enemy's stronghold. I don't fancy creeping round someone else's Camp. This one is quite strange enough for me. I can do some research while you are gone. Yes, that's it! I shall be a researcher. I shall like staying here with Merlin and the Emperor. You and Anir can go gallivanting off, if that's what you like, to risk your necks, if you like. I'll stay here. I'm just glad you have that you will have the Ring, Peter. I know you will need it."

Sarah swung round on the heel of her sandal in a sort of pirouette.

"You never know," she said, "I might even get to play chess with those wonderful silver chess pieces."

Peter studied his sister's face, he saw that she looked relieved. She really did *not* want to go at all. Sarah knew that the legionaries of Arthur and his allies were fearsome and in deadly earnest. The thought of meeting any more strange soldiers, especially those who would wish her harm, was just too much for her. She was actually more than happy for others to have this adventure.

"So then," said Anir, now it was all decided, "whatever happens, I suggest that you two get some rest. You have both had an early start, a double early start in fact."

"Does that mean we shall get 'jet lag'?" asked Peter.

"Probably. Merlin has told me that you may share his tent, as far as sleeping goes, but you shall eat at the table of The Lord Arthur. After all, you have both joined *the royalty* now!"

Anir made Sarah and Peter a mock bow.

"Merlin's tent is close to Arthur's, with those of his Officers, as you might expect. Come, I will show you where it is and you must both try to have some sleep."

Anir walked away and off to the left, behind the huge tent that was the Emperor's, and so to the one belonging to Merlin. Anir called Merlin's name and the wizard appeared at the tent's opening.

"Welcome to the tent of Merlin," he said, "there plenty of furs on the floor and silken cushions on my bed. Make yourselves comfortable and sleep well. Anir, perhaps you would care to rest here also?"

"I think I shall Merlin, thank you. Come on Peter and Sarah, you lie down on the bed and I will make myself a place on the furs by the door."

"Sleep well friends. I am going to see our young Emperor. We will expect you all to join us later on for Prandium, sorry, luncheon. Farewell."

With that, Merlin was gone. Anir lay down on the furs and slept straight away. For too many long years he had trained his body to the limits until now it did whatever he told it to do. Sarah was surprisingly glad of a nap and Peter also. It was partly the shock of their new surroundings. At home, only a few minutes had elapsed since they had left but Sarah felt as if she had lived an extra day already.

"Oh Peter, I do feel tired," she sighed, and fell asleep in seconds.

Peter pondered on what might happen next. Then he put it away from his thoughts and slept soundly.

The noise as of a bell out of tune being rung in their ears, woke all three travellers, shortly before midday.

"What in tarnation is that?" yawned Peter.

"I think they are ringing the gong for lunch, or Prandium, or whatever they call it. I am beginning to wish that we learnt Latin at school instead of French. It would be a lot more useful here."

Sarah stretched and got up.

"Hey ho!" she said, "they don't even know what French is yet do they?"

"I suppose it must be Gaulish," Peter said, "whatever that is, but I don't really know. I have never thought about it before."

Anir leapt up.

"Come on both of you, time to eat," he said, and hurried out of the tent.

Peter and Sarah followed him as quickly as they could because they were both feeling hungry again.

"I'm not going to enjoy this," Sarah said to Peter on the way to Arthur's tent, "I don't like hard boiled eggs."

"Just eat the fish and veg. then, and give all the eggs to me. I love them," said Peter, "and don't worry, you can always pig out on fruit, bread and cheese. They never seem to run out of those."

Anir tapped upon Arthur's tent post, as Merlin had done. A voice answered and they all went in.

The map table was covered with dishes. Osric stood to one side of it, holding an enormous pitcher of water. Arthur half reclined on a bench covered in the finest rugs and cushions, while Merlin sat bolt upright at the end of another bench.

"Never could get used to these *dashed* Roman habits," he said. "Thank you, Osric I shall take some wine as well as water today."

Osric obediently filled Merlin's cup and Arthur signed for his guests to join the meal. They ate hungrily. There were three courses and they were just finishing the third, when Gormant arrived unannounced.

"My Emperor, everything is ready. I think that we must leave now or we may not make Langres until tomorrow. I do not want to be outside that town in daylight, or for longer than is necessary. It would not do for us to be discovered."

"If you must, you must," Arthur returned, "you have our leave to go, and the blessing of our God and his Saints be with you."

Anir and Peter stood up.

"Are you resolved upon going?" Gormant asked them.

"We are!" both replied, with strong and unfaltering voices.

"Then we ride to Langres immediately. I give you my word that we shall return with all the information that you require, my Lord Arthur."

Gormant bowed to his half-brother and made his exit.

Peter and Anir grabbed their bags and bade a hasty farewell to Sarah, Merlin and Arthur. Then they left the tent to find a troop of the very best cavalry mounted in the Forum. Gormant was at his horse's side, waiting for them. The hot midday sun shone on their helmets and armour, their swords and their shields.

"Hail to our Emperor, Arthur the Great!" all cried, as Arthur came from the tent to receive their salute.

"And all hail to Gormant, Our brave leader!" the men chorused again, as Gormant leapt into the saddle.

Peter noticed that strangely enough nobody had stirrups, just like the Elves.

"You ride with me, young Peter," said Anir and straightway, he pulled him up on to his horse.

Peter sat in front of Anir so that he could cling on to the horse's mane.

"Away troops, To Langres!" cried Gormant.

105

"To Langres, To Langres!" the troops answered.

Sarah ran from the tent and waved as hard as she could. They were soon all gone from her through the fortified gate, in a great cloud of dust. Sarah was, and felt, quite alone.

"Never fear, little maid, we will look after you. Do not worry about your brother for he is in the best company. Gormant and his legionaries are very brave and I know that your Anir is too."

Merlin had come out from behind the tent and put a sympathetic hand on her shoulder.

"I'm not THAT little, thank you," pouted Sarah.

"We shall attend to all your needs while you are here nonetheless, whether you be big or little. You may stay in Arthur's tent now, until they call the evening meal. Gustatio, it is called here. I suppose you might call it dinner or supper. It will be a very grand affair this evening, because with Lucius and his army at Langres, we may take our ease, for tonight at least."

Merlin smiled, and pulled an egg from behind Sarah's ear.

"But I don't like eggs," she began.

"This one is different."

Merlin cracked the egg open, and out flew a butterfly.

"How pretty. Do you like butterflies a lot Merlin?"

"They represent ephemeral things, time passing, as I hope it will for you while your brother is away. When the spies return, who knows? We may have another big battle to fight."

"I do hope Peter will be alright."

"He will, I am sure of it."

Merlin stepped inside Arthur's tent. Sarah was surprised to find that Arthur was not there.

"He has gone to inspect his troops at their exercises."

Merlin answered her unspoken question.

"They must be drilled and drilled again, until their moves are perfect and their discipline under the Generals is entirely automatic. On this the survival of the Roman Legions once depended and on this the survival of our Romano-British Army now depends; that and the fact that we *always* have everything we need right here with us. We are entirely self-sufficient!"

Sarah was impressed. Then she asked about something which had been bothering her since their arrival.

"Merlin,"

"Yes, Sarah."

"Why is this Camp of Arthur's so dug in? I mean, it has a ditch and a huge fence on top of the earth ramparts, stakes coming out from the ditch AND a sort of wooden fort at each of the gates. Why is it like that when armies move about so much?"

"Armies do move about, Sarah, but this will be our base for quite a little while. We have come here from Mont St. Michael, and although the next battle may be in another place, somewhere convenient for an ambush, I hope..."

Merlin smiled darkly.

"we shall return here and probably not move again until next summer. If we are victorious that is, and I am fairly certain that we shall be, even though the odds are stacked against us."

"Are they?" asked Sarah, horrified.

"Oh yes, as I told you before, Lucius Iberius has thousands of troops from all over the Roman Empire. It will be the Golden Dragon versus the Roman Eagle again, just like the good old days before Claudius conquered Britannia in forty five AD."

Merlin rubbed his hands in glee. Sarah got the distinct impression that Merlin was one of the Old Britons who had managed not to be entirely Romanised. He certainly was a very odd person.

"In those days," Merlin went on, "Britons used to enjoy a good scrap with the Empire. Then *we* became the Romans and have been so for hundreds and hundreds of years. But now, when Arthur has finished here, it is the Invaders from the North that we must attend to. I am afraid that Vortigern, and others before him, made a big mistake when they invited them in to guard our northern marches. When we return to Britannia, Arthur and his troops will be older and wiser, and all the more powerful for being so. Arthur will have the strength to give those Saxons what they deserve.

Yes! Romans have been in Britannia for age after age. The Authorities may have gone now, yes, but those who remain keep hold of the glory they brought with them. The organisation, the buildings, our baths, the roads, the trade, (we still trade with Rome even now, you know!) our entire way of life, in fact. May it ever be so! Sorrowfully, I have to say that the Saxons, though colourful, have no respect for any of that. At all costs we must try to hang on to our civilised way of living. I would hate to have to do without baths, fine food, wine, glass in the windows and central heating.

Like the little butterfly I showed you just now, Sarah, our civilisation is precious and delicate. It is something we must nurture and protect at all costs. Sometimes, as now, I am afraid it is something we have to fight for. Then the only hope we have is that we have the greater forces, the better commanders, the more courageous soldiers, heavier armaments and God on our side. Ho, hum!"

The wizard yawned. Then he grinned a wicked grin at Sarah.

"In the old days, when it was the Romans that we used to bash up regularly, we had many gods on our side, positively hundreds to call upon; but then they did too. Was more the merrier or not, I wonder? They did not always seem to be powerful enough for the job in hand! We did not win against the Romans at any rate.

Now Romans and Ex-Romans all worship the same God. Constantine decreed it a long time ago. Although, now I come to think of it, the new religion came over just before the invasion of Claudius. There used to be a very nice Basilica belonging to it in the town of Silchester I believe. A friend of mine used to visit it frequently. Most faithful she was, my friend Drusilla.

Now none of us Britons, (well perhaps I should say: *hardly any of us*) use the old Temples to the gods. But in fact you could say that this God, the one that the Elves call the Power of All Powers, has been here longer than the Romans. Well then," the wizard laughed softly, "in a manner of speaking, I suppose He has *always* been with us... but whatever the facts; I sincerely hope that He is on *our* side now!"

"I hope He is too!" said Sarah, aloud to Merlin.

The Wizard looked at her sympathetically.

"And I hope He is with my foolhardy brother as well," she thought.

Merlin patted her patronisingly on the head. Sarah squirmed inwardly. She and Peter always hated grown-ups who did things like that!

"I must leave you now. I have a few things of my own to see to. Oh yes, and by the way, tonight at dinner you shall meet formally and properly two of Arthur's greatest Commanders; the Lord Kai and the Lord Bedwyr. They are two allies and friends of the Emperor of whom you *may* have heard in your own time. Rest well, take your ease, I will be back before dinner."

Merlin left Sarah feeling slightly irritated with wizards, but just a little more knowledgeable about the Roman Britons than she had been. She also wondered about Merlin's mixed allegiances: to the Romans, to the Britons, to their gods... or not. It was quite difficult to say what Merlin really thought about any of it. All that could be said was that he was obviously, deeply attached to his pupil and prodigy, Arthur.

The hours weighed heavy again. Sarah sat on of Arthur's benches inside the tent and wondered if she should go for another walk. She looked in the leather bag that Arthur had given her to hide her modern possessions. To her delight, she discovered that Peter had put the two books he had brought about ancient Rome in with her own things.

Happily she settled herself among some cushions and read for the rest of the afternoon. All was peaceful, save for the Sergeants or Centurions, or whoever they were, shouting at their men on parade. The warm summer breeze moved the skin walls of the tent and through the opening Sarah could see the brilliant blue of the summer sky in late Roman Gaul.

Peter had never ridden on a horse that went so fast in his whole life. He had thought that the Elves could go quickly but this... this was sheer madness. Gormant pushed his cavalry just about as far as man and beast could go, stopping once only to change horses at one of the old Roman Mail Stations that was still kept up by the locals.

"If this horse was in the National, or any other race at home, we should have won it by now," thought Peter, "Ooh! Oh! I think I might be going to be sick. I do wish that I hadn't had all those hard boiled eggs for lunch."

Aloud, he said to Anir:

"When do we get to Langres?"

"In the dark I hope!" said Anir, "Gormant will lead us as near to Langres as is possible. Then, the few of us who are scouts will go into the town, by one means or another. Once in there we shall be on our own. They will not be able to help us or rescue us if we get into trouble."

"Whoops," said Peter, "I think now that perhaps I should have stayed behind with Sarah."

"It is too late to go back Peter and anyway, you and I are not going to get into trouble. You have the Ring of Concealment, do you not?"

"Yes, of course I do Anir."

"Good. Keep it safe Peter. It is our passport in and out of Lucius' headquarters."

Anir urged his horse on again, even faster than before. Ahead rode Gormant and the elite troops that had been specially picked to go on this special mission. Peter thought of all the spy movies that he had seen on television. This was nothing like a film. It was much more uncomfortable.

"Ooooh!" he cried, as the whole troop galloped downhill yet again. "Aaaagh! this isn't the way I imagined travel abroad. Oh! Oh! Oh!"

And thus Peter complained all the way, until twilight crept across the sky and Gormant slowed the troops to a walk.

"We are getting close to our destination. Lucius Iberius will have guards posted everywhere. I would if I were he. We will walk from here on," Gormant said, dismounting.

All did the same. Gormant continued his instructions:

"When we arrive at the thicket to the right of the town's fortifications, you will all dismount. Those who are to go into the town will go on and find their way in. The rest of us will remain in the thicket. We will wait for the spies to return, but I warn you; as we told you when we made our plans, we ride at dawn. Anyone not here by dawn will have to make his own way back to Arthur's camp. That means no protection on the way. Do I make myself quite clear?"

"Aye, Lord Gormant," answered they all.

Then silence fell. The men and horses almost tiptoed into the thicket. Gormant tied his horse to a tree and gave it some food. A half dozen men grouped themselves together before Gormant. These were the spies. Anir and Peter went to join them.

"You know what to do?"

"Aye, Lord Gormant."

"The best entrance to Langres is by that culvert over there, to the left of the main gates. There is cover almost right up to the gates. Thank goodness Lucius has not had the undergrowth cleared from there. That means he must have a great deal on his mind. I would never leave something like that culvert so well hidden.

There seem to be several guards on the gate, so be extra careful. With luck, darkness and the bushes will hide you. Good luck when you get inside. Find out all you can. Don't get into any scraps. We don't want heroes tonight, we want information! Again, I say to you, BE CAREFUL, and Good Luck!"

The men turned their faces toward the town and Anir and Peter followed. When they all came within a certain distance of the town's walls, the men from Arthur's army got on their bellies and crawled along amongst grasses and under bushes, as quiet as hares.

Peter was just about to do the same when Anir took him by the hand, his left hand, the hand that wore the Ring. Very gently, he turned the jewel into Peter's palm and closed his fingers over it. Peter knew that now he must be invisible. Then, to his great surprise, Anir held on to his hand. With a shock, Peter saw Anir disappear also.

"We will go through the main gate," he said, whispering into Peter's ear, "you will be quite safe but you must *trust me*, and we shall then both put our trust in The Power of All Powers. Come on!"

Then, as silently as Elves, they crept forward towards the town.

CHAPTER SEVEN

The Raid With The Ring

"Nothing," Peter thought as his feet passed over the very threshold of Langres, "nothing could be quite so terrifying as this! Wondering, as you pass by the men guarding your enemy's town, if by any chance you actually are COMPLETELY invisible to them."

He looked straight ahead but even so, a glimpse of the roadway below made him uneasy. Did he see the slight possibility of his shadow, and the larger one belonging to Anir, shimmering away beneath him? There were huge torches burning at either side of the main gate.

"Like beacons they are, so bright, so bright. I'm sure those guards will see us any minute now!"

Peter felt a cold sweat break out on his forehead. His knees felt weak. A little more, just a few more steps and... thank goodness, they were through!

Anir pulled Peter at once behind the wall and away down a side street. When they found what seemed to be an empty shop, they flung themselves inside and crouched down under the counter. Anir removed his hand from Peter's and Peter could see him again.

"You needn't bother turning the ring, Peter, I can say what needs to be said without seeing you. We must get our bearings. I think, if this is a bakery, which by the smell of bread and the crumbs on the floor it must be, then I guess we are not too far from the Forum."

"Why?"

"Because the Forum is the central meeting place. You ought to know *that*, Peter, you being the son of an archaeologist! It will have all kinds of shops near to it, of course. It is rather like the towns at home that have a large market place."

"Oh, I see."

"Look, that very large building at the end must be the Basilica."

"It looks very broken down."

"Yes, I think that the troops of Lucius Iberius have been practising upon it what they hope to do to us later! Now there should be some large houses around here. Let us pass behind the Basilica and the portico over there and see what we can see. I must ask to close my fist around yours once more so that I also am concealing the jewel that will shield us from enemy eyes. Thus the Guardians and their descendants have learnt to use the

Ring in times of extreme emergency. Tonight there will be a curfew. That means any stranger found wandering about here will be slain on sight."

"What about Gormant's other spies?"

"Did you not notice Peter?"

"What?"

"They had changed clothes for some that the Goth prisoners were wearing. Lucius will think they are his own troops."

"Were some of them Goths? I didn't know."

"Yes Peter, many of them are Goths. Now come along, we do not have time to waste. Remember, Gormant rides at dawn, come what may. If by any chance we are separated, you make back for the thicket Peter, as fast as you can."

"Yes Anir."

Both closed their fists over the Ring and slipped silently into the darkened street beyond.

"I think that I am glad that they have not invented street lights here," thought Peter to himself.

Occasionally a lamp or candle glowed in a window, otherwise there were only stars to light their way. Anir was desperately hoping that they might chance upon the headquarters of Lucius sooner than later.

They crept on, behind the shops that were round the Forum. Around the back of the Basilica they went. Then, as luck would have it, Anir noticed a large building off to the right. The Villa had two stories and was obviously the domicile of some town notable that must had been requisitioned by Lucius and his Generals.

The Villa was full of light; lamp light and torch light. Obviously, Lucius and his officers did not see the need to be very secretive and were completely oblivious to the danger of the spies that presently walked the streets of Langres.

Peter and Anir were just about to cross over the street, when they nearly walked into two of Lucius' legionaries who were marching into the house. This made them fall backwards into a wine shop. Peter fell over a pitcher and broke it. Fortunately it was empty, but unfortunately the legionaries heard it break.

"What's that, Clementinus? I heard a noise. There shouldn't be no noises 'ere."

Both men looked around and naturally could see nothing.

"I reckon it's one of those cats them high-ups always like to have in their houses. Always getting out they are and making a nuisance of themselves, not to mention the horrible noise. Come on, there's nothing else here and the old guard have promised us a wet of the lips... if we get back smartish, that is."

The two soldiers then proceeded on their way.

"This is a piece of real luck Peter," said Anir, "we'll follow these two would-be drunkards and see where they go. Then I hope we may find out what we have come for."

They slipped quietly across the street, following the two men who passed through the gateway of the big house and down its main path. They kept well behind the two legionaries, trying all the time not to get too close. The soldiers turned off into the main part of the big house.

As Peter and Anir crossed the courtyard, Peter noticed how splendid the house looked with its roofed colonnade around the ground floors and the pool and fountain in the centre of the courtyard, or atrium.

The soldiers came to a halt. They saluted two others at the front door of the house and then went off to the left, down a corridor. Peter and Anir passed swiftly by the old guard who kept their station, then followed the others down to a room at the end of the house. As the soldiers entered, they were greeted warmly by at least one other, and bade to sit down and have a drink before going on duty.

"They are being rather careless," Peter thought, "which is something I had better not be!"

Anir and he slunk into the shadows at the end of the corridor. There was a window with a ledge. Anir pulled Peter over to it.

"You wait here, Peter, I am going to scout around a bit. I am going to try and see if I can get a look at any of their maps or plans. I'll be back shortly. If I'm not, make for the city gates and get out."

He did a back flip out of the window and disappeared into the night.

"How brave he is," thought Peter, who had rather put Anir upon a pedestal as Hero for the duration.

Someone definitely to be imitated, if at all possible! Peter then remained seated, silent and still like one of the statues in the garden. There he waited for about twenty minutes upon the window-ledge, listening to what passed in the room beyond.

"Well, well, Clementinus, and how's the world with you?" their host began.

"All right, I suppose," said Clementinus.

"Oh, you'll feel a lot better after some of this. Good Gaulish wine this is. I've had half a pitcher myself already, so I know it's good! Hic!"

"He's drunk!" thought Peter, "and he's going to get the other two drunk as well, if they are not careful. And they're going on guard duty shortly. Well that'll be good for us. Perhaps they won't notice us leaving."

With this pleasant thought, Peter settled himself down to listen again.

"Now then, now then, Gaius Maximus, have some more of this; do you good. Hic!"

"I can see it's done you a lot of good already," said the first soldier, "I tell you, I need a bit of this. Oh, it's not like the good old days. You knew where you were with the Legions then. My father and his father before him, they were both in the army. Good life then it was, (Slurp!) plenty of the spoils of war and the odd slave to had out of it, and retirement with a pension when you'd served your time. Now what do we get? I ask you?"

"Only he isn't really asking them," thought Peter, as the soldier drank deep of the wine, he's going to tell us the answer himself. This is a bore, I'm getting nothing out of this."

"I ask you," continued Clementinus, "we get pushed from pillar to post by this rotten Proconsul..."

"That must be Lucius," thought Peter.

"From pillar to post, and on behalf of one of these usurping, upstart Emperors wot has no more right to our Glorious Roman Empire than I do."

"They don't seem to like him either, that's good," mused Peter.

"Well, let's make you Emperor then," offered their host, laughing.

Gaius took up the complaint.

"Yeah! And tomorrow we got to march back where we came from, back to Autun! It was one of Lucius' own bodyguard told me, just before we goes marching round this Langres place on guard duty.

First we gets ordered to Autun. Then we has to fight those slimy Britons. Then we chases after them 'cos they got some of us prisoners. Then we does an ambush, but the Britons fight back. Now we're in this hole and nitwit Lucius can't make up his mind what to do next. Whether to ask the Emperor in Rome for reinforcements or not. Now I gets told that it's definitely back to Autun again. Wot we're going to do there I really don't know, what with only half the forces we ought to have and would have had too, in the good old days."

The soldier sniffed pathetically.

"I bet Lucius will go to Autun, stock up with provisions and prepare for a siege. That there Arthur and his Britons will never

118

attack us during the winter, they're not brave enough," said Clementinus, leaning forward.

"Nah! Never were," agreed their host.

Peter felt himself flush with anger. How dare they, how very dare they say such things. He nearly fell off the window ledge with indignation, but managed to pull himself back in time. After all he, Peter, knew that Arthur would be remembered *for ever*, even if it was not quite for the right reasons, or apparently, the right story. No-one, however, was going to write romantic tales or make movies about a certain Lucius Iberius and his upstart Emperor, Odovacer.

"Well lads," said the host, "I'm feeling sleepy. I'm not on duty again until dawn, but you are, you two reprobates! Out you go and don't let one of these darned Britons get the better of you. You've had enough courage out of a bottle for one night."

"We're off!" said the two soldiers, who were by this time distinctly unsteady on their feet, "and just you remember; no sleeping in! We want relieving on time, we does."

And off they went to take over the guard.

"What did those advertisements say during the Second World War?" Peter asked himself, "ah yes: 'careless talk costs lives', that was it. Well this little chat is going to cost them plenty, IF we manage to get this information back to Arthur."

He was about to move from the window, when the old guard appeared round the corner and went in to the guard room. Peter could hear snoring. When the others went in they were most scornful.

"He's nearly drunk it all," they said, "and those other two! They'll be flogged if they are found out... if they're lucky!"

And so their complaints went on. Anir returned and pulled Peter off the ledge.

"Anir! I've heard *all* their plans," whispered Peter.

"And I have managed to get a squint at some maps," said Anir. "I think we have both done well, but now it is time we went."

He closed his fist over Peter's, and they slipped past the guards who were definitely not as alert as they should have been. Thankfully they passed out of the courtyard. Peter looked back. The grand house was almost dark now, all save the soft glow of lamplight coming from one of the upper windows. It seemed likely that someone was wakeful, possibly even Lucius Iberius himself.

Peter felt curious. He wondered what Lucius was like and what he was planning up there in his room. Anir brought Peter down to earth. He pulled him away and they sped across the street and down the side of the forum, narrowly avoiding a large patrol of Goth soldiers. Then Peter recognised where they were. They were in the street of the bakery again.

"Look Peter, there is a faint glow in the sky over there. We must hurry now so that we are back in good time."

They passed quickly down the street. A chill breeze was blowing. The guards by the main gate were marching up and down and slapping themselves in order to keep warm. It was quite a feat, dodging in and out and in between them, but at last Peter and Anir were back among the bushes and undergrowth. They were out of the town, out of Langres and on their way to meet Gormant and the others in the thicket.

When they arrived, Peter turned the Ring. All those gathered were as still and as silent as could be. The pale light of dawn showed in the Eastern sky. Without a word, Gormant made a sign and all mounted their restless horses. Anir and Peter discovered that they had been the last to leave Langres and were therefore lucky that the others had waited. Gormant gave another sign and the troops moved slowly and quietly off; riders like shadows in the half-light of dawn. They passed through trees, bushes, scrub and undergrowth, until after a while they came to a rough road. They were by this time about a mile and a half, maybe two miles from the enemy encampment.

"We might risk going a little quicker from here on," Gormant called back.

He pressed his horse from a trot into a slow canter. The others followed suit. Then when they were a good six miles away, Gormant urged his horse into a full gallop. From then on, because it was after dawn, they went as fast as they could; only slowing to a trot occasionally. Rests were taken only when absolutely necessary. They had a slightly longer rest at midday by a river, where the horses could be fed and watered. All the horses were *lathered up*, but there was no time to rub them down properly. Their riders were only able to walk them round a little, hoping that would be enough.

After their horses were attended to, the riders were able to eat their provisions. No one talked very much. They were all too tired and too concerned about getting their vital information back to Arthur. Peter told Anir everything that he had heard in the Consul's house. Then he felt so tired that he would have liked to have gone to sleep right where he was. He threw himself down on the grass, but Anir picked him up.

"No sleeping on duty! We still have a long way to go. You can rest properly when we are back in Camp."

"But I want to go to sleep now, Anir."

"No!" said Anir firmly and put Peter straight away back up on his horse.

Then, two minutes later they were off again, chasing Gormant who rode like a mad man. In fact, it was well after dark when they stumbled wearily into Arthur's Camp. Peter was all but asleep in the saddle, but he and Anir were hurried away to the Praetorium immediately to make a first, if rather brief, report. Arthur was overjoyed and very impressed. The raid had gone much better than anyone had hoped and the spies had garnered much useful information. Anir then carried Peter to Merlin's tent where he was laid upon the bed amongst the furs and cushions. He fell at once onto a deep sleep.

Moments later Sarah came from dinner, which had gone on rather late, to join her brother. She was greatly relieved to see him return unharmed, and was soon asleep beside him. Anir went with Gormant and the others to meet with Arthur. It was nearly dawn again when they slept at last. A Counsel of war had taken place. Plans had been made and decisions taken.

Next morning, Peter and Sarah woke late. Life in the Camp was already in full swing. They knew that they must have missed breakfast, but Peter still had some food in his bag, leftovers from the day before.

"I'm so glad you're back in one piece, Big Bro."

"Not half as much as I am Sarah. It was really, *really* scary and the enemy H.Q. was absolutely crawling with soldiers. We certainly needed that Ring of Gyges. We could never have managed without it. And Anir; Anir was great. I'd trust him to the ends of the earth and back, from now on, for ever!"

Peter lay back among Merlin's rugs and cushions and felt glad to be alive.

"I am so glad, Peter, I'm so glad you're back with me," Sarah said and all of a sudden she gave him a big hug.

"Oh, well, er!" Peter muttered, and blushed.

The curtained opening of the tent moved and Merlin's head appeared.

"Good morning little people," he said, "wide awake I see. Ready for action, I hope?"

"Ready'ish, I suppose," said Peter, still feeling rather tired.

"Sarah jumped up.

"I'm ready," she said.

"Come with me then please. Arthur wants to see you."

He swept off out of the tent and the children followed him as quickly as they could. Two minutes later, they were in the tent of the Emperor Arthur once again. The young leader looked as bright as a button.

"Welcome, fair cousins! And I gather that you well deserve the title, Peter, from what Anir told me last night. Well done! You deserve The Golden Laurel Wreath at the very least! It is you alone we have to thank for the information that Lucius is leaving Langres for Autun."

"Gosh, Sire, thank you!" said Peter, and blushed even redder than when Sarah had hugged him.

The Emperor Arthur's blue eyes sparkled with pleasure.

"Yes," said Peter, "I heard the guards in Lucius' headquarters discussing it. They did not seem to be very pleased about marching all the way down here again."

"Well, it is wonderful news for us," said the Emperor, "we have all agreed the time and the place already!"

"The time and the place for what?" Sarah blurted out.

"The great ambush! The battle to end all battles! Come over here."

Arthur pointed enthusiastically to the map on the table.

"Look here, between Autun and Langres there is a valley through which our enemies must pass if they are returning here. I have proposed setting our divisions here, here and here."

He pointed to various spots on the map.

"I and my division will remain here. We will all be on the higher ground to the south east. Lucius will come from the north west, down the valley."

"Doesn't that mean that he will be facing into the sun?" asked Peter.

"Aye, it is an old soldier's trick, but none the worse for that. They will have difficulty aiming their arrows and javelins at us and they will not see ours coming at them until they reach their mark. Lucius is mistaken if he thinks that he will reach Autun unscathed. And you, Peter, heard the guards! A really excellent piece of spy work, if I may say so. But now..."

Arthur looked round at them all.

"Now the greater work begins. Today we fight. We shall beat Lucius and all his army. Then we shall march on Rome and beat the Emperor Odovacer as well! He is a usurper and an upstart and does not deserve the title of Emperor, any more than I do..."

Peter wondered if the young man was thinking what he was thinking. Why should not Arthur of the Britons make a bid himself for the highest estate of them all? Why should *he* not become Roman Emperor?

"It would be wonderful to see Rome," Sarah said suddenly.

"Aye, it would indeed," agreed Arthur.

"Can we go with you?" asked Peter.

"First things first," Merlin broke into their dreams of glory, "Arthur has to win the next battle before he even thinks of going anywhere near Rome and the Emperor!"

"Oh Merlin, you are so pessimistic," said Arthur.

"And you are too easily inclined to optimism. Ah! I suppose it is one of the faults of youth. However, if you prepare well, organise your troops properly..."

"They are organised, Merlin."

"Organise your troops properly and plan for every eventuality, you may win the day. For of course, it is the events that you least expect to occur that are likely to upset you. For example, what happens when it all goes wrong? Hmm! If Lucius does not come down to Autun, you will sit on your hillside all day for nothing. Or, suppose he has many more troops than you expect, or..."

"He hasn't, the spies have counted them; he doesn't, he won't! In fact I happen to know from the scouts, that the enemy is on its way right now. Stop trying to make me feel depressed Merlin.

Whatever happens, in half an hour from now, all our troops; well almost all, will march forth from here to the valley of Saussy."

"Half an hour!" cried Peter and Sarah in surprise.

"Yes indeed, half an hour. In fact, I can hear the Ensigns forming their maniples and the Centurions forming their centuries up right now, and if I am not mistaken, here are my brave Generals coming to agree last orders."

In strode Gormant, Kai and Bedwyr; then King Flergant and Lord Kaw, Gyssevin, Arthur's Champion and Henwyneb; then several more whom Peter and Sarah had not seen before. These included some officers from the Danes and Norwegians. The Gauls were well represented and the Bretons also, not to mention local chiefs from all over Britain. All met in Arthur's tent to plan the great battle against the Romans.

They were to bypass Autun, leaving it to the left and going on to the valley at Saussy. One Legion, besides Arthur's own, was to remain in reserve. The remainder were to be divided into seven divisions; each to contain five thousand, five hundred and fifty men. The exception was Arthur's own Legion, which was to comprise nearly seven thousand men. All the Legions were to have two Commanders.

"I guess there's one for the infantry and one for the cavalry," (which made up the greater part of Arthur's army) Peter said, in a low voice to Sarah.

Sarah was beginning to feel incredibly nervous. She remembered the battle that they had been in with the Elves against Arddu, the Dark One! She remembered that it had not exactly been an enjoyable experience. She didn't really wish to see another one. Nervousness made her giggly.

"Where do baby soldiers go?" she asked Peter, prodding him in the ribs.

"I don't know," Peter said absently, for he was intent upon what the Generals were doing.

"Into the INFANT-RY, of course," giggled Sarah.

"Ssh!"

"Where does the General keep his armies?" Sarah giggled again."

"What?" said Peter, who in his mind was still attending to other things. Sarah repeated the ancient joke.

"What? Oh, on a hill, I suppose."

"No, silly, up his sleevies! He! He!"

"Oh Sarah, do shut up! Look, I think they're getting ready to go."

All the Generals bowed themselves out of the Emperor's tent. As they went out Anir came in.

"The troops appear to be ready to leave. May I relieve you of the children?"

He beckoned to Peter and Sarah and they went to stand by him.

"Yes, thank you Anir. Merlin will accompany you and the children, won't you Merlin."

"Yes, I expect I shall, though I do not enjoy fighting. However, I have sharpened my own sword in case of emergency."

"Very good. Then I am off to lead my army to battle. Onwards to Saussy and Victory to the Britons!"

Arthur passed out of his tent, leapt on to his waiting horse and:

"Raise the Golden Dragon! To Saussy and Victory!" he cried. The whole army took up the cry:

"To Saussy and Victory!"

The Emperor Arthur's standard was raised. The Golden Dragon gleamed and sparkled in the summer sun. Arthur rode forward out of the camp gates and the huge army of the Britons and their allies followed him. To Saussy they went, and hopefully to the winning of the battle!

CHAPTER EIGHT

The Battle of Saussy

Anir placed Peter in front of him on the horse, as before, and Merlin took Sarah. They just had time to pluck their belongings off the floor before being swept off to ride behind Arthur and his Golden Dragon.

"When is lunch?" Peter asked, as Anir walked his horse in line with Gormant, Kai, Bedwyr and Merlin.

"Hmmm! It is about ten o'clock by the sun. I think that Arthur will not stop before we reach the battleground. He will want to have his troops well in place before Lucius gets anywhere near the valley. Surprise is always a good weapon."

"Oh!" said Peter, greatly disappointed.

"Never mind about your complaining stomach," said Anir, with a laugh, "I have the ultimate secret weapon."

"And what is that?"

"A full saddlebag, naturally. And if you were wondering, Merlin has one too. Everything has been most excellently prepared down to the last and smallest detail. The King-Emperor is nothing, if not thorough. He leaves nothing to chance, whatever Merlin might say. That is part of what makes him a great leader. He also cares for his men and shows that he does. That means they will do absolutely anything for him. He is young and fit, and I suspect incredibly strong, judging by the size of his muscles. I think this army would follow him to the world's end."

"I don't think I would like to be this Lucius Iberius," said Peter, "but what about the saddlebag?"

"Oh Peter! When the sun reaches its overhead position, then you may make a raid upon the bread cakes, a full attack upon the cheese and make prisoners of the apples. Thus you will score a victory over hunger. There now, does that answer your question?"

"Yes thank you."

"Good! Enjoy this great sight then. I am sure you will not be among such Great Ones again for a long time to come."

Anir pushed his horse onward, just a little bit, to keep in line with the others.

Sarah had her own questions to ask.

"Merlin?"

"Yes Sarah."

"Merlin... are we, Peter and I, to be at the battle?"

"I am afraid it rather looks like it, but not too near to the fighting, if I have anything to do with things."

"When will they begin to fight?"

"Very early tomorrow I expect, assuming that Lucius and his army actually arrive in the valley by then."

"I don't think that I want to see this battle."

"Most understandable, neither do I," said the wizard, frowning. "I have never been able to get on with this 'joy of battle' all these great hulks go on about. It is all so uncivilised, walloping ones opponent until he, or you, are in bits!"

"No, I think it's perfectly horrid," Sarah agreed, "can't we get out of it? Can't you take us somewhere else? But not home, not just yet, I want to see if they win," she added hastily.

"Well, I'll have to think about it. In a strange way, you are probably fairly safe as long as you stay near to Arthur. However, I at least will have to stay near our noble leader for most of it, just in case he needs me."

"Oh, but that would definitely be cheating, wouldn't it? I mean, using magic to win."

"We already have. And it is not really cheating at all. You see Sarah, we do not know for certain that the enemy does not employ a magician for their side. In fact, in these days it is highly probable. More than likely, I should say. So very wisely... Arthur keeps me tucked away for emergencies!"

Sarah's mind leaped to her own small emergency.

"I'm awfully hungry, Merlin, when do we eat?"

"When we get there. I am expecting the cookhouse to prepare us something really splendid to go out on. An army marches on its stomach you know. But..."

Merlin paused, as Sarah's face had fallen to uncharted depths at the thought of waiting any longer for something to eat.

"if you reach inside the saddlebag to your left, yes, that's it! I have prepared some snacks for you and I in the meanwhile. You did not think that I was going to miss my luncheon, did you? Certainly not! Just pass me some of that delicious bread and cheese, will you."

They munched on Merlin's snacks. Sarah noticed some of the generals and other soldiers glaring at Merlin. Oh well! If he did not care and apparently he did not, then Sarah did not care either.

The army went on. Because about half of it was infantry, they had to go slowly. Then too, in the mighty column, there were many wagons and machines of war. Apart from one short rest, they marched on all day, reaching the valley of Saussy at twilight. Mists were forming on the valley floor.

"That is good," Arthur commented. "It will make our forces less easy to see, less easy to count when Lucius arrives here. We will take the higher ground as we planned, up here to the south of the valley. Gormant," he called, "Gormant, have the scouts ready in half an hour, I must know where Lucius is now."

"Aye, Lord, it shall be done," said Gormant, and he went away to see to it.

Meanwhile, the whole army prepared to make camp for the night. As in the days at the height of the Roman Empire, ditches were dug, ramparts appeared and stake palisades sprang up all around them. Tents were being put up everywhere, horses were looked after and the cookhouse, as Merlin suggested, prepared a feast for the men. Quite a few more farm animals had apparently been requisitioned on the way to Saussy and they were quickly made ready for dinner.

Eventually, Arthur's Legion came to dine and Peter and Sarah found each other. They stayed close to Anir and Merlin.

"I thought the Romans ate things like dormice and thrushes and nettles," Peter said, as he chewed a chicken leg.

"So they do still," said Merlin, reaching over for a nice juicy lamb chop, "but less so than they once did. I think you will agree, this is preferable. In general, we save delicacies like dormice stuffed with olives and garlic, and lark pie for extra special feasts. Ho there, Osric, ask Kai to send more bread down this end, will you; and tell Bedwyr that we could do with some more wine."

"I always thought that Kai and Bedwyr were great knights," said Sarah, "but one seems to be in charge of food and the other in charge of wine. Why is that, Merlin?"

"But my dear Sarah, they *are* great knights. Though to be Cup bearer or Overseer of the King's food is a very great honour also. They are two of the most honourable positions at court. You should see us feast, when we are at Gelli Wick! Yes, these positions are like..."

"Like running all our royal palaces at home?" asked Sarah.

"Something of the sort, I suppose," Merlin replied, "now do be still, Sarah dear, eat up and let me pay attention to this very fine pitcher of wine."

Sarah realised that Merlin wanted to be quiet, so she wriggled a little closer to Peter. He was trying water with his wine.

"I'm not sure I like it," he said, making a face, "this wine is a bit too dry for me, but it is all there is. I would much rather have a cola, but we are fifteen hundred years too early!"

"Never mind, I'll get Aunt Myf to buy you a case full when we get back."

They were both silent for a minute or two, thinking of Aunt Myf and Gwyn-ap-Nudd waiting for them at Arx Emain. They would be watching the time and waiting for the moment to call them back.

"I make the time twenty minutes past three," Sarah said casually, winding her watch up.

"Yes, so do I. That means we've got, Ooooh! Days left. Good, I really want to see Arthur win this battle, now that we've come so far with him. It would be a pity to miss it and I have to say, sister dear, I wouldn't mind having a go at Lucius Thingy myself."

"Ugh Yuk!" Sarah said, "I don't know how you can even think that, you bloodthirsty thing. If I get the chance to get away, I shall. I'm telling you; if we ever come on another adventure... let's make it one without a battle in it, PLEASE."

"Well I want to see him win," repeated Peter, "I'd rather like to join in and even if I don't, I want to know if he goes to Rome."

"I must admit, I should like to know that too. In fact, if this Emperor Arthur does go to Rome I should like to go with him."

"Not much chance of that, Sis, we've got two days with Arthur at most, enough to see his battle won but not enough to see the war won. Anyway, at the end of two days, either Aunt Myf, Gwyn or Merlin will call us back. Still, you never know."

Peter turned around. Arthur was seated behind them, with Anir, Gormant, King Flergant and Lord Kaw. Bedwyr and Kai, when they were not organising the feast, were also seated close to their Lord. Some of the other commanders were walking through the lines of soldiers to Arthur's place and as the meal was nearly finished, they were obviously going to have yet another meeting.

"Let's go away from here," Sarah said, "I haven't seen you properly since Langres. Arthur seems to think you have all done a good job there."

"OK, we'll go a bit further up the hillside, and yes, we jolly well did do a good job. Good? It was nothing short of miraculous! Look Sarah, sit here. Aren't the stars clear. Yes, I shall tell you all about what we did in Langres."

And so they talked of their experiences apart. When Peter had finished his tale, Sarah proclaimed that she was most impressed. She had had a quieter time in camp, but had also found out this and that. Sadly, they would never meet Gwyn-ap-Nudd's kinsman, for he had been killed during an earlier skirmish with Lucius Iberius.

"But apparently, he was one of Arthur's very bravest fighters," Sarah said, "I'm sure Arthur will try to get Gwyn-ap-Nudd on his side when he gets home. I also discovered that when he is at home, Arthur spends his time moving between several palaces. I suppose it helps to keep any enemies guessing! One of his main Halls is in Cornwall, somewhere that I've never heard of before, a place called Gelli Wic. It is a huge place, Merlin was boasting that it has nearly fifty rafters in the main part, is richly decorated and is very grand. It is one of Arthur's favourite Halls.

At Christmas, Easter and Whitsuntide, or as Merlin says: Nadolig, Pasc and Sulgwyn, they hold a great feast wherever they are staying; Merlin mentioned Caerlleon, Penrhyn, Tintagel, Chester and some other places. It depends what Arthur is doing at the time. AND... get this Peter! The Round Table isn't a table that you eat at, at all! It's some kind of meeting place they have, near to Arthur's Halls. By the way Merlin describes them; I think they *might* be the old Roman Amphitheatres for the Old Games. I found out that Arthur is called *Emperor,* because that's the nearest thing to the Welsh, or British name that he has, which is: *Penrhaith,* or Supreme Ruler!

I am awfully afraid that there does not seem to be a Camelot either, and no Sir Lancelot. Merlin says that they must have been made up in later times. Maybe you're right and the Normans did make that up. He says that *he's* never heard of those names anyway and he ought to know. He did help to bring Arthur up, though. That is why they are such good friends. Merlin will do absolutely anything for Arthur. He's been jolly kind to me too while you were away with Anir. Sometimes he gets a bit crusty and grumpy, but that's just his way. He doesn't suffer fools gladly. I like him!" Sarah yawned. "I don't know what the time is but I'm tired."

"And I'm doubly tired, after being up all night in Langres. Do you want to have the Ring again? I nearly forgot to ask."

"No thanks, Big Bro. You keep it for a while. If you get embroiled in the battle tomorrow, you might need it. I'm going to make sure that I stay right away from that! Anyway, I had already decided to give it back to Anir ages ago, just as soon as every thing is finished here."

"All right then Sarah, I shall keep it for the present. But I must get some sleep."

So they curled up right where they were on the hillside, with a couple of bushes at their backs for shelter, and fell asleep.

Dawn came slithering mistily over the hill tops. The Camp was already awake and most of Arthur's troops had been moved into position during the night, as had range after range of catapults and balistae, together with many lines of archers. Arthur's Legion, and the other reserve troops were to stay on the hillside, to be constantly at the ready. The Emperor would remain with them until required, probably after the first phase of battle was over. The other seven divisions had already received their standing orders. Each Legion comprised both cavalry and foot soldiers, with the emphasis on the cavalry. When the foot soldiers moved forward in the standard square position, then the cavalry were to come forward obliquely with closed ranks and charge the enemy.

Peter and Sarah woke up with a start. Trumpets were clamouring and Merlin was shaking them.

"Up, up, little people! The enemy is here and Arthur has set up his Golden Dragon against the Imperial Eagles and standards of Lucius Iberius."

"Where is Anir?" Peter asked, rubbing the sleep from his eyes.

"Where's breakfast?" asked Sarah, putting first things first.

"I am afraid that breakfast occurred two hours ago," replied Merlin, "for today you will have to rely upon what provisions I have managed to glean. Leftovers from the feast and from this morning's breakfast they are mostly. I am afraid the cookhouse is well and truly shut for the duration of hostilities. As for your mister Anir, he is down there with Arthur, right next to the Golden Dragon. You must keep right out of it today. You can watch from here, if you want to... but you are not to go down into the valley. Those are the Lord Arthur's strictest instructions; your standing orders if you like."

"I'm not sure that I do like," said Peter, "I wouldn't mind joining in..."

"I like it , I like it!" said Sarah quickly and positively.

And so they stayed as far up the hillside as possible, for Merlin would not let them go further down. Occasionally he went down himself to see how things were going and if Arthur needed any assistance of the supernatural kind! But in the main he did not. Peter and Sarah watched as the preparations for battle progressed. The Lord Arthur and his Generals passed through the lines of foot, cavalry, artillery and the archers, everywhere proclaiming the battle motto of Arthur's Legions: "Might and Justice!" to hearten the troops and lend them courage.

The men were tense and ready to start. The catapults were wound up, the ballistae armed. Centurions and legionaries stood with pilum and gladius at the ready. Arthur's cavalry and the auxiliaries reined in their horses which were straining at the bit, ready for the charge, all on horseback having their spatha, or long Celtic cavalry sword, unsheathed. Merlin looked upon it all with a satisfied smile.

"Did you like the mists this morning?" Merlin asked them rather sheepishly.

"Yes," Peter said, "but I thought they were natural."

"Oh, they were," said Merlin, "I just thickened them up a little, so that the enemy would not see us until the very last minute. I didn't want Arthur's 'battle boosting' speech interrupting. He gave the most rousing discourse I have ever heard from him. It

135

nearly made me want to go and thump Lucius myself and that is saying something I can tell you!

He is a most determined young man, our Arthur. He says that we shall be *off* to Rome; just as soon as Lucius' head is... OFF, I mean. Well and so, Peter and Sarah; we shall see what we shall see. Oh look, I think they are about to start. They are getting ready. Dear me, I think they ought to be very, very careful with that burning pitch. Look, the balistae are primed and their javelins are raised. AAAND... they're away!"

Arrows and catapults rained down their fiery projectiles upon the enemy. Then the legionaries pressed forwards. First they threw the pilum, then they went forward from behind the safety of their shields stabbing with the gladius. The cavalry charged, causing confusion among the enemy ranks and assisting the infantry in their attack.

"I think the Britons look better organised," Peter said, after the first charge was over.

"Yes," said Merlin, "I don't think Lucius' Senators have their troops quite under control yet. Our surprise has worked. They also seem to have more infantry than cavalry. That could turn out to be a mistake. Mark my words, young Arthur knows what he is doing in that respect."

Peter decided that the army of Lucius Iberius looked odd.

"Why are there so many different uniforms and different looking people among Lucius' troops," he asked.

"Because, my dear boy," Merlin said with just a hint of exasperation in his voice, at being asked so many questions all the time, "the Roman army of today is not what it was. I imagine there are hardy any real Romans left in it now. Strange to tell, I think that this may be one of the last times that the Roman army fights as it used to do. I do not think that they have the same will for fighting any more. That is why the invaders are getting the upper hand; that and other things.

Anyway Peter, as far as I know, the Roman army has been propped up with barbarian auxiliaries for years uncountable! The Romans always did have many foreign forces, but now I think they wildly outnumber the true Roman legionary, altogether and completely. Also, you may notice that their legions are a lot smaller than ours, and thank goodness for that, I say!"

"Thank goodness indeed," agreed Peter.

"Which ones are the Senators?" asked Sarah.

"Oh, can't you tell? They are the ones with the most highly decorated uniforms and gold inlaid swords. The ones over there, riding grey horses."

"Oh yes, I see them... But only just. Hey! I have an idea. Look, Merlin, I've got these in my bag."

Sarah brought out the tiny binoculars and showed them to Merlin. When she had described how to use them, he was thrilled.

"By the Heavens!" he said, "these are useful. They are almost as good as my magic. Can you lend them to Anir? He can be scout for the day and help young Arthur see what is going on. If I give them to Anir people will think that they are just another of my magic tricks and ignore them. What a pity that they are not invented yet. Never mind, it is something I might work on later." Merlin dashed off to give the binoculars to Anir.

"That's good," said Sarah, " I think that means that Anir will be kept out of most of the fighting. I should not like anything to happen to him. I have got rather fond of him. I think I quite like old Merlin too."

"Not so much of the *old*," said Merlin, coming up behind them suddenly. "Arthur appreciates your gift. My words! You two are proving to be useful. I don't think we can let you go home now, not after all this. What else have you got in those bags I wonder?" his eyes twinkled and they knew he was joking.

"Wow," said Peter, looking down into the valley again, "I'm afraid a lot of the Romans have had it. The Britons are really getting through now. Look Merlin, is that Lucius Thingy over there?"

"Yes, Peter, it is. The Britons have got right through to his personal bodyguard and he and his friends are going all out to assist them."

They all watched as the battle went to and fro. The Britons and their enemies charged, fought, reformed and charged again. The day grew hotter and hotter. The fighting in the afternoon was very bloody. The noise was frightful. Sarah could not bear to watch any of it, as it was all too much for her. She took herself off and went under a bush right at the top of the hill. There she read the school library books on Ancient Rome.

"Well, at least I shall know more than Peter does when I've finished reading all this," she thought, trying with all the determination she could muster to concentrate on the books.

Peter remained with Merlin. Arthur had not yet gone to fight himself, for as yet it had not been necessary. The King-Emperor stood apart, with some of the other senior officers and his own personal bodyguard, waiting to see what should pass. Peter wished very much that he could have gone and been a part of it all, even though he had to admit to himself that he found it quite terrifying.

Twilight came again. Both armies ceased fighting in order that the wounded should receive attention and the dead receive decent Christian burial. Over the evening meal, Peter and Sarah discovered that among the dead were Kai and Bedwyr. This made Arthur very sad and the Britons in the troops belonging to the great leaders, very angry. Most of them went about saying that they could not wait for the next day, in order to revenge the deaths on Lucius' troops, and probably on Lucius himself.

It was a most uncomfortable night, hot and humid with no wind. Peter and Sarah were glad to be sleeping outside. It was also unpleasant to be in the presence of the enemy, who though they had sustained heavy losses, looked as though there were more than plenty of men and spirit left to fight.

The next morning, the sun shone hotter than ever. This made tempers hotter and thus the fighting hotter! When the battle began again, the Britons had the worst of it to start with. Lucius Iberius had had all night to make plans and this day he was more than prepared. Some Britons tried to get to Lucius and failed. Then King Flergant, Gyssevin and Gormant attempted to get through Lucius' personal bodyguard. Eventually, Gormant found an opening, rushed forward and fought Lucius hand to hand. However, while Gormant and Lucius were locked in mortal combat, the rest of the Romans had time to recover themselves and began to attack King Flergant and the Bretons.

"Oh no," cried Peter, "look Merlin, the Romans are beating back King Flergant. Gormant and his troops; they're falling, they're falling back! Oh, this is awful."

"I think I had better go and advise our young monarch," said Merlin, sounding anxious, "what ever happens; stay here!" and he disappeared down the hillside as fast as he could.

Seconds later they saw Merlin by Arthur's side. Then they saw Arthur with a great cry, draw his famous sword Caledvwlch from its scabbard. His legion roused themselves, they followed the young Emperor in a magnificent charge. He fell upon the enemy like an angry lion.

" No prisoners!" the angry cry went up.

"No prisoners!" they heard, as Arthur at the head of his troops, dashed down upon the enemy, cutting to pieces any who were in their way.

The Britons were seeking revenge for their fallen comrades and leaders. All the Britons and their allies charged the Roman

Eagles once more, attacking them in close formation. Peter and especially Sarah, were shocked and surprised to see Arthur and his troops behave in this way, but Peter thought he understood...

The Romans fought back as bravely as they could, Lucius Iberius at the front of the fray. Fearful slaughter occurred on both sides, I am afraid to say. Then, in the end, one of the British Generals brought down some of the troops who had been kept higher up in the hills for extreme emergencies. They swept down and attacked the Roman rearguard.

Peter became very excited. He insisted that Sarah come out from her hiding place to look. She had disappeared with the books as soon as she heard the trumpets bray that morning at dawn and he had not been up the hill to speak to her since. Sarah was an unwilling spectator.

"We're going to win, we're going to win!" Peter cried, jumping up and down. "See Sarah, over there, they don't know what to do! The Romans are scattering. Look, there goes another Eagle and I can't see any of their Senators. I think someone must have killed that Lucius Iberius. Some of them are giving themselves up and others are running away. Hey, Merlin, is it over? Has Arthur won?"

"He has, young Peter, thanks be to God and the bravery of our troops; and just a little thanks to you and me, I think."

He took Sarah's binoculars from a pocket and gave them back to her.

"Is Anir alright?" Sarah asked.

"Anir is alright! Thank you for asking."

Anir strode up the hillside and stood before them. There was, however, a rather deep gash over one eye and a cut to his thigh. He held a large piece of cloth.

"Will you bind these up for me?" he asked, and handed them to Sarah, who did her very best.

She had once done a first aid course as a First Aid Cadet, but that had only been practice; this was the real thing.

"Well done Sarah, thank you," said Anir, "I think, if you did not mind doing that for me, there are others below down there you know, who need your skills."

"That's OK, Anir, I'll go," said Sarah, and ran off down the hill.

"You can go and help too, Peter," Anir said, as he sat on the ground to ease his wounds.

So Peter followed Sarah down to the valley where the wounded were collecting. There were some people acting as doctors in what seemed to be a makeshift sort of a hospital, but they didn't seem to know very much and so were not really much use. Sarah did her best and a good best it was too. She did not seem to notice how awful everything was, but went straight to work. Peter assisted her, but he had to admit that she was much better at bandaging up wounds and comforting the patients than he was.

Even with the most basic of modern first aid practice, Sarah managed to do better than the army doctors. They seemed to have forgotten much of what the Greeks had passed on to them in former times, when the medical service in the Roman army had been second to none. Later, Merlin came to the Hospital also and did very well, though he swore that he knew nothing about doctoring. Sarah thought it must be his great knowledge of anatomy and herbal remedies that stood him in such good stead.

And so the day of the Great Battle at Saussy came to a close. Gormant, Gyssevin and some others went away after a hurried meal to round up what Romans had not escaped, or surrendered. Many were taken prisoner, but many were also killed.

"It's a good job they did not enter the town and have us lay siege to Autun," Arthur said later.

"Why?" asked Peter.

"Because then we should have had to kill every last one of them, and indeed everything alive in the city, that's why."

"Yuk!" exclaimed Sarah, horrified.

"But that has always been the Roman way and everyone knows that. They would not hesitate to do it to us if our positions were reversed. Say, if they had laid siege to us in our camp. That is what happens if you do not surrender immediately. Once the battering ram touches the gates... well, I'm sure that you remember what happened to Archimedes!"

Peter and Sarah did not remember, but they presumed that this was exactly what had happened to Archimedes.

"Poor guy!" said Peter, with great feeling.

"Poor Syracuse!" said Merlin, sourly, "you know Arthur, it might be good to contemplate on the thought that, just because something is a Roman tradition, it is not necessarily a good thing!"

There was a very strange atmosphere in the Camp that evening. Many were joyous because they had won, but there were those who were sorrowful because so many were lost. The evening meal was a dismal affair because Kai and Bedwyr were gone. Although Arthur's champion, Gyssevin, did his very best to fill both their roles.

"I shall have to bring him on in the ways of the Cup bearer and Butler," Arthur said, "he will come to it by degrees I am sure."

"And what will you do now, my Lord Arthur?" asked Anir, as dinner drew to a close.

"Rome, Anir, we will go to Rome in the springtime. We shall spend the autumn and winter here and then cross the Alps when the snows are melting. I can't wait! Then we will give that Emperor Odovacer a bloody nose for sure, either on our own account or more probably, in alliance with Theodoric of the Eastern Roman Empire."

"Very good, Sire, but first we have much clearing up to do," Merlin said.

"Yes Merlin," the young King-Emperor said, "I know, I was getting carried away."

"It is the foolishness of youth to think they can achieve ALL," said Merlin, dampeningly.

After that, the meal finished very quietly and all present were glad of some sleep.

CHAPTER NINE

Ancient Rome

Early next morning Arthur's army began to prepare to go back to the camp by Autun. The battlefield was cleared. The wounded were placed on wagons and the dead laid to rest. All except Kai and Bedwyr, who were to be buried in their own home towns in Britain and northern Gaul. Solemnly, their followers left Arthur's army with their sad burdens.

Arthur was not ashamed to weep at the sight.

"They were the truest of friends and the bravest of Generals. Farewell Kai, farewell Bedwyr," he said as the corteges moved off.

"Thank goodness that's over!" said Sarah. "I can't stand unhappy endings."

"But we haven't got to the ending yet," Peter replied, "we have at least another day here, then another night, then we'll have to go."

"I'm not sure I want even one more day."

Sarah turned her back on Peter and sniffing rather, began to walk away from him.

"Hey! Come on Sis, don't be like that..." and Peter caught up with her, put his arm round her and gave her a big hug.

At length Merlin found the dispirited pair. He had come to call them to join the long march back to Autun. Sarah rode with Merlin once more, but on this occasion Peter was given his own horse to ride. They took up station between King Flergant, Kaw, and Gyssevin, who smiled at them in a most friendly way, agreeing that Peter and Sarah had done well. Anir was with the wounded on one of the wagons.

Only one stop was made, this was in order to tend to the wounded and to break for the midday meal. Then the slow cavalcade went on to Autun and the Camp by the river. When they arrived, Peter and Sarah were surprised to find guards on the gates as usual.

"Not all the legionaries went to war," Merlin said in reply to their questions, "surely you did not think that our brave Arthur would leave his Camp undefended. What would he do in case of retreat? No, he leaves nothing to chance, and in fact no General worth his salt would his home base unguarded."

"Of course, I see that now," said Peter, feeling slightly stupid.

Strangely their spirits seemed to rise as they rode through the fortified gates. During the evening, Camp life began to return to normal. Those who had survived were glad that there would be a winter and early spring to come before they moved on again. Crossing the Alps would be very difficult, even if the snows on the passes did melt.

Never mind, when they got to Rome it would all be worth it! They would win more battles, gain much in booty and spoils of war, especially if Arthur beat the Upstart Emperor. Whatever might happen then was anybody's guess. Perhaps Arthur himself could become Emperor of Rome. The Romans themselves would have plenty time to ponder on this, as Arthur had sent the body of Lucius Iberius back to them, proclaiming that it was the only tribute that they could expect from the Britons.

Spirits lifted! By the time of the evening meal the atmosphere in the Emperor's tent was positively buoyant. Osric served the meal and poured the wine, and made a good job of it. All the generals were at dinner and Anir managed to stagger to the tent also, in spite of his wounds. Merlin and Anir were very jolly. Arthur sat back among the cushions and listened, while the heroic deeds of his troops became grander and grander as the wine flowed.

Sarah and Peter left the party early with Merlin. They did not feel as ecstatic as the other guests of Arthur. They knew by the time on their watches that Gwyn-ap-Nudd was likely to call them back at any moment.

"Dawn at the latest," Peter declared sadly, "only a few more hours to go, Sis."

He did not know that Merlin was listening intently to their conversation.

"I wish we could have seen Arthur marching into Rome itself," said Sarah, "THAT would have been a grand sight."

"It would indeed," the wizard replied.

Then he suddenly became most animated. Jumping from foot to foot, he said:

"Let me see, when do you think you departure is scheduled?" he asked as the children made themselves comfortable among the furs on the bed.

"About dawn tomorrow," said Peter mournfully.

"Just a moment then. Yes, I have it!" cried their friend, "Go to sleep, go to sleep Peter and Sarah. I have just had the most amazing idea. I have surprised even myself! Yes, go to sleep. Do not worry about the dawn, I shall be back by then with some good news I hope. Goodnight," Merlin said and was gone.

He fairly shot out of the tent and returned to the Praetorium. Unfortunately, Merlin's tent was well out of earshot, so Peter and Sarah had no idea of what passed next. They were soon in the land of nod and missed Merlin's discussion with Anir and Arthur and the drawing of the triangle in the air. Then there was the sudden disappearance of Merlin yet again, and his reappearance seconds later with a large grin from ear to ear.

Dawn came. The crimson light crept into the tent. Peter and Sarah awoke to find Merlin standing in the entrance of the tent and smiling at them. They were astonished to find that they were still in Arthur's Camp and showed no signs of being pulled back home.

"We're still here," said Sarah , brushing the creases out of her Roman style tunic.

"So I see," said Peter, "what's afoot, Merlin?"

"It was Sarah who gave me the idea last night. Your visit with our young Emperor, though informative and at times dangerous, if not exciting; may not have been at all times entirely enjoyable. To make up any failure on our part, I have been on a little journey of my own. I have agreed with your Aunt an extension of the time limit and a little extra entertainment."

"Aunt Myf!" cried Peter and Sarah.

"Yes, I took the opportunity last night for a brief visit. Now I know how to open the door, it is quite simple. I was going to take

Arthur through it at least once anyway, before we return to Britain at last. I thought that after all the recent unpleasantness, we could all do with a holiday."

"Oh Merlin, that sounds wonderful! But how long have we got, and where shall we go?" they asked him eagerly.

"I am afraid I have only won you half an hour more of your time, but that will last us until this evening. Then we will definitely have to say farewell to you. As for where we shall go, isn't it obvious? I am taking you and Arthur to Rome. It will be most educational for the young victorious one also!"

"Oh Merlin, you're a darling," said Sarah.

"Wow, that's really neat," said Peter, but what about Anir?"

"Anir I have sent back to Arx Emain. His wounds are not too serious but could do with the attention that only Aneryn and Gwyn can give to them. However, I did bring someone else back with me to see you in his stead. If you come with me now to Arthur's tent, you will find breakfast, a visitor and afterwards a day out in Rome."

Merlin then led two very excited children out of his tent and into that of Arthur. In the Forum, Legionaries were forming up for drill as usual.

Merlin tapped on the tent pole. A voice said:

"Come, I know it's you, Merlin."

They went inside, and there was the greatest surprise of all. Standing next to Arthur, already changed into Roman clothes, was:

"Aunt Myf!" Peter and Sarah gasped.

"Hello Peter, Sarah. I see you have survived all right. I'm afraid I am a glutton for punishment. When Merlin asked me if I would like to come on a jaunt, I just couldn't say no. It is wonderful to meet such a hero as King Arthur."

Arthur actually made Aunt Myf a very small bow.

148

"And of course the prospect of a day trip to Ancient Rome, well, what could I say but yes?"

"I'm very glad you have come, Aunt Myf," said Peter.

"And so am I," Sarah agreed.

"Well then, you had better eat and then we'll go, shall we Merlin?" Arthur asked smiling.

Osric brought breakfast, which was eaten very quickly. Peter and Sarah were eager to tell Aunt Myf all their adventures. Occasionally, Arthur or Merlin would prompt them and breakfast became most good humoured.

At length, Merlin said that they could delay no longer. Gormant was summoned and told that that he was in charge for the day. Arthur said that he was going on a special scouting mission with the children. Gormant left them, mystified but obedient to Arthur's wishes. Merlin prepared to send them all through the doorway that the power of the Stone of Gardar had created.

Briefly they all saw the land of the Summer Stars, then the tunnel of light and in seconds they were safely set down in the Eternal City. The Stone had put them behind a pillar, somewhere on the Palatine hill.

"Now everyone," said Merlin, as they wandered down towards the Forum, " Listen to me! Just for today we are a Roman family. I am Pater, you Aunt Myf shall be Mater, and I am afraid, my Lord Emperor, that from this moment on, you now have a younger brother and sister. That is our cover, if any one should ask. They probably won't. Everyone looks very busy here. It looks as though we have arrived on Market day. If we get into trouble we can go back through the Door, but you must all stick to each other like glue. Arthur, you especially must remember that if you get lost, it is along walk back to your Camp from here!"

"I will not stray too far, I promise, but what a wondrous place this is. Though it is not as glorious as it once was, I can see the

149

greatness of it shining through. It looks as though all the armies in the world have been through it. It is very much broken down, poor Rome," said Arthur.

"But," Sarah said, "You can still see how wonderful these buildings must have been in their prime. Where do you think we are, Merlin?"

"My guess Sarah is that we are quite near to the Roman Forum, which is the oldest. Of course it got too small eventually, and several of the Caesars: Julius Caesar, of course, Augustus too, Trajan and Vespasian built themselves other ones. Look, there is the Citadel defending the north of the Palatine. That ought interest you Arthur, there are enough fortifications there to satisfy any number of generals."

"Thank you, Merlin, I'll remember that," smiled Arthur.

The sun shone bright in the skies over Italy and the Romans went about their business, taking no heed of their strange visitors.

"Come along, come along everyone," Merlin hurried them along as if he were a tour guide, "there is a great deal to see and to wonder at. Rome wasn't built in a day and I don't suppose that we can see it all in a day, but we may try and take in the most important points."

They were now standing by a magnificent archway, which Merlin said had been put up by the Emperor Titus, the eldest son of the Emperor Vespasian. From this vantage point the time travellers could see right down over the Roman Forum. It was from there that Merlin took the trouble to advise them about what it was they were gazing at.

"Look, there are market stalls put up in what is left of the Basilicas. That one was built by Julius Caesar, the other used to be called the Basilica Aemilia and the big one over there was the Basilica of Constantine. There is a church in what used to be the temple of Antoninus and Faustina now and I'm afraid the temple of Castor and Pollux does not look as proud as it once did when it was used for important meetings of the Senate. Eventually, they used to meet in that building there, Sarah, the old Curia. Then, years ago, this whole area was filled with lovely monuments and great statues too. The temple of Vesta kept the Sacred Fire and the temple of Saturn kept all the wealth of ancient Rome.

Look above on that hill. That is the Capitoline Hill. What is left of the Temples of Jupiter and Juno stand there; together with the Tabularium, where they used to keep all the state documents."

"Don't you mean parchments?" asked Peter.

"Or stone tablets?" added Sarah.

"Maybe even wax ones," replied Merlin impatiently.

"And from where did the great Orators speak?" Arthur asked his tutor.

"From over there, I think... I think that is where the Rostra used to be. You can just imagine it, Cicero himself perhaps, standing up there before a mighty crowd:

"Cedant arma togae, concedant laurea laudi," or in English..." began Merlin, for they had been speaking English amongst themselves the while, in deference to Aunt Myf. Merlin had arranged the instantaneous translation personally!

"Let arms yield to the toga, laurels to eulogies," completed Arthur, "or I suppose you *could* say triumphs or victories, instead of laurels."

Merlin smiled broadly at Arthur; the satisfied smile of the teacher who sees that his lessons have not all gone to waste.

"I am gratified to find you have retained something of your boyhood lessons," smiled the Wizard.

"Yes, and I take note of the lesson of your quote," replied Arthur, "you can't wait for us all to return to civilian life, can you!" he said with a slight growl.

"Well done!" exclaimed Aunt Myf, in admiration, "I only got half of it, but then it is a long time since I was at school. I don't

151

think they teach Latin to the boys and girls anymore..." she looked at Peter and Sarah, who shook their heads.

They had not understood any of the strange words, although some of the sounds seemed strangely familiar. This was not surprising, for their father, Dr. Jones, was often having to translate Latin during the course of his work and not only that... so many Latin words had made their way into the everyday language of Peter and Sarah that they were bound to recognise at least some of them.

"A very great pity," Merlin said, "for I believe that the ancient languages ought always to be studied, in order that we can hold on to the lessons from the past and so press forward with proper knowledge into the future."

"Agreed," said both Arthur and Aunt Myf.

Sarah and Peter were not too sure on this point!

"What language do you speak at home?" Sarah asked Merlin.

"Why the ancient language of the Britons, of course," replied the wizard.

"Or Latin," added Arthur, "in fact, at Court, mostly Latin and some Greek. All Romans used to speak Greek as their second language in the old days, you know. We do use our own language sometimes, but most often when we are being private, or just within the family."

Arthur sighed a heavy sigh, remembering past lessons.

"I had to spend many years learning Greek and Latin grammar before I could speak fluently," he continued, "it would not do for the Supreme-Ruler of Britannia to be unable to communicate with the rest of the world, now would it?"

Sarah and Peter were impressed. The Emperor Arthur was certainly an extremely well educated young man.

Merlin walked swiftly onwards.

"I think if we turn this way, we shall come to the Imperial Palace, what is left of it, the Domus Augustus, and there too is the

Domus Flavia, which used to be the centre of all imperial activity. Also, beside the Colosseum there are the remains of the Domus Aurea, the Golden House, which was Nero's palace. We shouldn't miss that if we can find it. The Stadium is quite near also."

"How do you know all this ?" asked Sarah.

Merlin just winked, and whispered :

"Perhaps I have been here before! And perhaps I inform myself by reading. I am not *THE* Tutor to our young British Emperor here for nothing you know!"

"I think it all looks magnificent, fabulous, wonderful," Peter remarked, "and so much of it is still standing. In Father's guide book much more of it seems to have gone."

"I am sure that will be the effect of one thousand, five hundred or so, years of young generals like Arthur here, coming along to knock even more of it down!" said Merlin, frowning.

"Very well, my old friend; I know you keep trying to make me agree with your point of view. I am beginning to change my mind about various things. I'll shall certainly think hard about what you have said."

And Arthur remained quiet for some time, walking at the back of the little group, while Merlin continued their tour.

They walked down the Via Sacra, The Sacred Way. Sarah never forgot that walk, for two reasons. One was the magnificence of the road that entered the Forum, it was all massive stone slabs. The other was the extreme heat as they toiled down into the Forum itself. She wished they could have had sun hats, as they usually did when visiting abroad.

"The Romans call this *the oven!*" said Merlin, casually.

"And I can see why," said Aunt Myf, "it's positively airless down here."

"No wonder the Caesar Tiberius used to go and live on Capri in the summer," Arthur remarked, "I would have done too, if I were he."

They were thrilled by the Temple and House of the Vestal Virgins, especially to find so many statues still there of the priestesses, each bearing the name of its subject underneath. In fact there were so many temples to this god and that, Peter's head began to reel. It was hot so they all had to have a drink from one of the magnificent fountains.

"Which temple did you say this was, Merlin?"

"The Temple of Castor and Pollux, Peter. It has been here in one form or another since the fifth century BC, you know. And there is the Arch of Augustus Caesar, and there is the one belonging to Severus. Come along Sarah, or you will get left behind. You must keep up, all of you. Oh do come along!"

And so they passed the many famous and fabled sights. Merlin pointed out various ancient churches that were built upon the ruined temples of the old Roman gods. Everywhere there were beautiful statues and columns. Particularly interesting to Arthur was Trajan's Column, with its depictions of military campaigns around it.

They walked and walked. Peter and Sarah vowed to each other that if, or when they came to Rome in modern times, they would come in a coach or hire a scooter.

Lunch was bought in some shops near one of the Forums. In a bakery, Arthur made a most interesting discovery. As they chatted to the baker's assistant, they discovered that the Emperor Odovacer was away campaigning in the north of Italy, known in these times as Cisalpine Gaul. Arthur had heard whispers to that effect, but had not heard all the details.

Odovacer, who had taken the Roman empire over by force in a most unpleasant way, was now having to defend his claim in real earnest! Theodoric, the favourite of the Eastern Roman Emperor had now been sent by Leo to get rid of Odovacer, permanently! It was the general opinion in Rome, so the baker's assistant informed Arthur, that Odovacer was most likely to lose his throne to Theodoric.

"Although it is Goth against Goth," he said, "we're backing Theodoric, for he has the might of Emperor Leo with him."

When Arthur reported this conversation to Merlin, he added: "And I think I shall definitely go and help Theodoric! It is obvious to me now that *Odo-face-acher* just wanted tribute from us Britons in order to fight off this threat from the Eastern Empire. Well, Merlin, I have made my mind up! I was going to cross the Alps anyway, and even if we don't come as far as Rome itself; for the Emperor's palace is at Ravenna I gather, it would be good to know that I had helped to beat Odovacer. I know it would please all my troops and our allies and give the people at home great satisfaction. Yes, this has helped me to make up my mind... we march in Spring!"

"Splendid, my dear Arthur. And now that you have seen Rome itself?"

"I have seen it! It is marvellous, the most strange, marvellous, fantastic and glorious place I was ever in. I certainly have no wish now to add to the sackings of it. However, if we could assist Theodoric in making the Roman Empire strong again, then we in Britannia and indeed all the citizens of the Empire, would feel safer. If only Rome were powerful once more with a firm leader, I am sure we should not be so troubled by all these Invaders."

"Good, I hoped you might say that. I am very glad to hear that the remains of these beautiful buildings have nothing to fear from you! But I this I say to you, Arthur: a strong and powerful Roman Empire may be something for which we all might keep having to wish and pray about for a considerable time to come. However, our little visit has not been in vain, I think," Merlin smiled, "and now, onward, dear friends. We have the Colosseum to visit next."

Once there, the time tourists took quite a while to marvel at the Colosseum, the arena having the capacity to hold at least fifty thousand Romans at once, or maybe even more!

"It is so much bigger than I imagined," exclaimed Aunt Myf.

"Wow! It's humungous. Just think of the Gladiator fights they used to have in there," said Peter, "they must have been fantastic!"

"And don't forget all the poor Christians they used to throw to the lions either! All totally disgusting and gruesome," said Sarah, "just like you, Peter."

"It must have been exciting, though," said Arthur, joining in, "all the beast hunts and the battles! Otherwise there would not have been copies of this place right throughout the whole Empire. Why, there is even one close to one of my homes; at Caerleon, in fact."

"Well, I don't like to think of it," said soft hearted Aunt Myf, "it's too horrible. Those poor people: the slaves, prisoners and Christians who died in there! We might have been in their shoes if we had been there in those days. *We* might have been thrown to the lions!"

"And in this time; *my* time, or *our* time, I should say," remarked Merlin, including Arthur in his conversation, "those days are not all that far away. Much too short a time to be comfortable in fact. It was not until the time of the Emperor Honorius that Gladiators were finally banned in **404**. That is only *fifty years*, more or less, before you were born, Arthur my lad!"

This was a very sobering thought and left the time travellers quiet for a long time.

"Where do we go next?" said Arthur at length, feeling that enough inspection had been made of that dreadful place.

"The afternoon wears on apace," replied Merlin, "I think we shall finish with the Basilica Church of St. Peter. Then I am afraid we shall have to bid each other farewell."

Sarah then looked so downcast at this remark that they had to try and cheer her up somehow.

"We have about four hours left, at least," said Aunt Myf encouragingly, "Merlin, shall we not pass by that nice little market by the Forum over there, we might get something to eat and drink."

"I have an idea," said Peter, "why don't we all find something to take back with us. After all, we can't be proper tourists unless we have a souvenir."

That gave everyone something to think about, and all kept their eyes peeled after that for some small trinket.

They found a shop selling fruit and vegetables, near the Forum and bought dates and grapes. All felt cheerful, if a little weary, as they approached a bridge over the river Tiber.

"This is Nero's bridge," announced Merlin, "we must cross here if we want to see the Church and I know that Arthur does."

Arthur nodded in assent.

"I have always wished to come there as a pilgrim," he said.

Then at last they came to St. Peter's Basilica.

"A much humbler building than the one that we know in our time," Aunt Myf said, "but then of course it was greatly built up and added to in the sixteenth century."

The Basilica had been sacked by yet another Goth; Alaric, in 410 AD. One could see there were many signs of damage, though a brave attempt at repair had been made.

Arthur was resolved to go inside to pray at the tomb of the Apostle and Aunt Myf and the children said they would go also. It is not every day that one can get to walk by the bones of the greatest fisherman ever!

They were all struck as they entered, by the peace inside the Church and stayed there for a long time in silent contemplation.

Sarah thought of St. Peter. They had recently gone over his story at school. She thought of the rough but enthusiastic fisherman, who had been chosen by the Lord to leave his humble occupation by the lakeside and had thereafter become a fisher of men. In that capacity he had been drawn to Rome which was then the very centre of the whole world...

In some ways, it was still the centre of the world, though in quite a different manner than before. A new Roman Empire had taken the place of the old... one that was still global; even though it was now more spiritual than temporal. Peter was thinking of the name that Rome is often known by: The Eternal City!

"It's true," he thought, "it's all still there for me in *my time*, or most of it is."

Over a thousand years forwards in time, it was still there. You could see its mark on almost every city in the whole of the civilised world. Peter cast his mind back to the towns he knew at home. Banks and other grand and important buildings had Roman columns at their doors. The reinvented architecture of the Palladian style, with its colonnades and porticoes, meant that there were still many, many places around today that made his homeland look as if the Romans had been gone but a little while.

Then too, there were all the thoughts and ideas that had been carried forward to Peter's time; important ideas that needed to be nurtured and built upon if, according to his father and Merlin too, mankind in the future was to become truly grown-up. Yes, the Glory of Rome might be diminished now, but hundreds and hundreds of years later; *it was still there!*

As the King-Emperor Arthur knelt on the well worn floor of the Basilica, Peter wondered what he was thinking. What would a recently victorious Emperor be thinking of? The next campaign perhaps, or was he hoping for peace?

Sarah got up from her place on the floor and walked back towards the doors, disturbing Peter's train of thought. As silently as he could, he got up also and followed her out of the Church, leaving the Grown-ups a few more minutes of peace.

Time was running out however; even though, when they all emerged back into the golden Italian afternoon, the sun was still high in the heavens. As the evening breeze from Ostia ruffled Sarah's hair, she knew that she had definitely fallen in love with Rome.

"I do hope we come back... I hope I will come back," she whispered.

Peter's watch showed twenty minutes to six o'clock. Merlin made his preparations and seconds later, the familiar sounds of the Camp of the Britons could be heard. The Emperor Arthur took them back inside his tent. Aunt Myf, Peter and Sarah went to the trunk which held their modern day belongings and clothes. With great reluctance they changed their dress and got ready to say *goodbye*.

"Very strange you look to me now, fair cousins," Arthur said to Peter and Sarah, "we have gone a long journey together in more ways than one, these last few days. There is just one question that I should like to ask you before you leave..." he said, looking quite serious, "Shall I be famous in your time?"

What were they to say? For Arthur has been, and still is, and will always be famous. But not for what *really* happened or for what he *really* did. Though of course, Peter and Sarah assured him that he definitely was a very famous person in their time!

"You will be known as a really GREAT King," Sarah told him.

"People will tell many, many stories about your adventures," Peter added.

"And I haven't seen off the Saxons yet," smiled their royal friend, "that is something for us to do, Merlin, when we all get home."

Peter and Sarah could see that what they had said pleased the young King-Emperor.

"But just remember Arthur," Merlin said, "the Caesars were, or is it, are really famous rulers and look what happened to them. They are all gone and their glories with them. Let that be a warning to you, Arthur my boy!"

"Merlin, you are like the slave who stood behind Caesar at his triumphs, whispering: *remember you are mortal*. But I take your warning as good advice. I will do my very best not to become big-headed, I promise."

"It is nearly time, Peter, Sarah and Aunt Myf. Are you ready?" Merlin asked.

"We are," they said.

"Thank you, dear Merlin and Arthur, for having us in your great adventures," said the two children.

"That is quite all right, it was our pleasure," Merlin and Arthur replied.

"Will we see you again?" asked Sarah.

"I do not know," Arthur said, "perhaps you may. We shall have to wait and see."

Sarah thought she saw the air begin to swirl.

"Goodbye," she called.

"Goodbye," called Peter and Aunt Myf.

Then they all lost sight of Merlin and Arthur and the tent and the Camp. Both Peter and Sarah felt rather sad.

They were standing once more in the Room of the Stone, with Gwyn-ap-Nudd seated on his throne before them. The Elf King was smiling broadly at them.

"Welcome home," he said, "I called you back. It is six o'clock precisely," he said. "I see that you, Sarah, and you, Peter, have survived the journey. I hope you have enjoyed the experience."

"Oh we have; we did!" exclaimed Sarah ecstatically, "thank you very much Lord Gwyn!"

"I also *trust* that Peter has *passed The Test?*" continued the Lord Gwyn, looking at Peter hard and long, "in fact, I know that you have! So don't worry Peter, I have already spoken with Anir. I must say, you certainly look as if you have done well, which is what The Guardian has told me in his report. We look forward very much to greeting you here again *very soon* Peter... and Sarah too of course, whenever you wish to visit."

Sarah curtsied to Gwyn-ap-Nudd and Peter bowed to the Elf Lord. Peter wondered silently about the Elf King's remarks to him.

Deep down in his heart there was now the firm and definite stirring of a hope that one day he, Peter Jones, might possibly get to know the Elves of Arx Emain as well as Anir apparently did. Again, he remembered that it had been soon after the great battle with Arddu, when he had first began to wonder *where* the Guardians came from and why and how. It was, he realised, just after he had used the Stone of Gardar to call forth the Samildanach during the great battle, that he had begun to feel different; changed in some way.

Although his normal life had then carried on as usual, Peter now began to think that the future might be going to turn out very differently from the one he had imagined for himself only a couple of years ago. He no longer thought that he would be joining the Firemen for a career, or even that he might be an archaeologist like Dad!

This *Test* that the Elf King had just mentioned and which he had somehow managed to pass, almost without noticing, must obviously be something to do with all the nods and winks from Gwyn and Anir. All at once, he began to hope very much that it was. Then too, Peter knew that Gwyn had read his mind, seen into his very soul. Indeed, as the Elf King looked at him, he appeared to be doing it again right now, probing and searching all the boy's innermost desires.

"To be The Guardian of Arx Emain... what a dream *that* would be," Peter was thinking.

...And the Elf King *must* know it! However, Peter decided to keep the whole thing a deep and deadly-dark secret, until he had got onto firmer ground with it, so to speak. No-one, not even Sarah must know what he was contemplating.

Then he noticed that Aunt Myf smiled a knowing smile at Gwyn-ap-Nudd. What did *she* know about anything? She certainly was the most mysterious of Aunts! And although he tried hard later, Peter was unable to gain any further information from her... for the moment!

"Thank you my Lord Gwyn, thank you for everything. I would love to stay a little while longer, but we shall have to leave directly," Aunt Myf said, leading the two children backwards towards the doors of the Hall, "Uncle Tomos will be waiting with Catrin. You know how it is, my Lord."

"I do indeed," replied Gwyn.

"But first, can we not see Anir?" asked Sarah, "I *would* like to know if he is all right."

"Me too!" said Peter.

"A brief visit then," said Lord Gwyn, and a few seconds later, Morvith appeared in the doorway.

"Come with me," she said.

They followed her down the corridor to a room near where Peter had once been placed, when under the enchanted sleep. When they entered, Aneryn was sitting on a stool beside Anir, who was asleep.

"Ssh," she put her finger to her lips.

"Is he all right?" asked Aunt Myf.

"He will be all right. He just needs some rest, that is all. I promise, next time you come he will be well."

"Then we will go now," said Aunt Myf, "come on children, home time. Goodbye for now, Aneryn, Give our regards to Anir when he is awake."

"I will, Myfanwy, farewell!"

Aneryn waved them goodbye.

All ran back to the Room of the Stone, thoughts of upset or annoyed relations filling their minds. By the power of the Gardar Stone, the Lord Gwyn was kind enough to return them to the bus stop. Aunt Myf's little car was safe and sound, to her great relief and she may be forgiven for driving a little quicker than usual on the way back to Newport.

The rest of the weekend was a real anticlimax, save for the moment they emptied their rucksacks and found the souvenirs they had collected while in Rome. Peter had picked up a coin with the head of one of the Caesars on it. Sarah had found a small pottery dish. They were most excited about their finds. When the coast was clear, they went to see what Aunt had brought. They found her in the kitchen, giving Catrin pulverised Sunday lunch. Uncle Tomos was resting in his study; which meant that he was asleep.

"What did you get, Aunt Myf?"

"Pardon?"

"From Rome, what did you bring back?"

"Oh, I found this tiny little statue. Someone must have dropped it near one of those temples that we looked at. Very nice, it can go in my display cabinet."

"But," Peter and Sarah looked at each other, "Dad will see it and he will know what it is. What will you say if he asks you where you got it?"

"The same as you, when he sees your finds. Tell him the truth, why not? Tell the truth and shame the Devil, as they say. Either he will believe you or he won't. Now look at you Catrin; you are dribbling all over the place again."

Peter and Sarah took their finds back upstairs. When Father collected them on Monday he remarked how quiet they were.

"I have some good news for you both," he said, "Mother is coming back to us on Friday."

Then the rest of the week became a whirl of activity, to make the house ready and tidy for Mother's return. Friday came and they collected her from the station.

Grandmother had returned home much improved and her neighbour promised to keep an eye on her. The following day, Saturday, it snowed.

"How strange it is," mused Sarah, as she and Peter looked out upon the strange, grey, white world.

"This time last week we met King Arthur and Merlin. We fought battles, went on missions and visited Ancient Rome, sweltering in the hot summer sun! Do you think we shall see them again, Peter?"

"Who, Merlin and Arthur?"

"Yes."

"Who can say Sarah. Oh, I nearly forgot, I still have that Ring. We didn't get the chance to give it back to Anir. Do you want to keep it? I asked you before, wouldn't you like it now?"

"No thanks, you keep it for the moment brother mine, I've had quite enough magic for the present thank you very much! I do like this little dish, though. I think I shall keep it on my dressing table."

"OK Sis, I'll keep the Ring for now, but we will give it back to Anir as soon as we can. Look, I have this nice coin with the head of a Caesar on it. When I get time I shall look it up in one of Dad's books downstairs."

They told Father all about what had happened, after supper that evening. Then they had to tell Mother. What their fond parents said to them at first was fairly unprintable! Then they said that they were going to have very strong words with Aunt

Myf. Then Father was so pleased with the coin and the dish that the children had brought back that they were almost forgiven everything.

Later that year they were in Rome again, for the *dig*. But it was not the same. Peter and Sarah enjoyed watching the students working with Father. In fact they were most helpful. Everyone was so surprised that two young children, not yet at secondary school, should know SO much about Ancient Rome.

"But after all," the students said, "their father *is* an archaeologist, a Professor, no less!" and so they let it drop.

But some of the students remained suspicious, especially at certain times, when Peter would wink at Sarah, and Sarah would wink at Peter. Then they would chant a little ditty in Latin, which Father had taught them, before going off into peals of laughter:

HIC STABAT ARTVRVS
REX IMPERATOR FVTVRVS
IN VRBE AETERNO ROMANO

Here stands Arthur, the once and future King.
Here in the Eternal City that is Rome!